Preparing an Operatic Role

Preparing an Operatic Role

Legendary Italian coach Ubaldo Gardini and leading opera artists on the approach to a convincing vocal performance

To Peter & Georgina
with best wishes
from
Marie Myerscough

MARIE MYERSCOUGH
WITH FOREWORD BY SIR COLIN DAVIS

Published by
WHZ Books
11 Gloucester Walk
London
W8 4HZ

First published in 2008

Typeset in Sabon Roman by SCW
Book designed by SCW - www.scw.uk.com
Printed in the UK by JFDi Print Services Ltd

ISBN 978-1-903872-24-6

This book is dedicated to the memory of
Ann Hummel (1943–2007)

FOREWORD

Ubaldo Gardini was a unique character. Those of us who were lucky enough to work with him during his years at Covent Garden learned more of *bel canto*, Italian and Mozart than we could have thought existed.

He had both an inexhaustible energy and a fund of knowledge, which could often wear his colleagues to a ravelling. But they took away with them as much as could be known of vowels (open and closed), double consonants and liaisons – plus how to keep them all from 'cutting off the voice' and therefore interfering with the true *legato*, which is the gift that singing renders to its devotees.

Ubaldo was a violinist by training and a mandolinist for fun. He was also an expert on Italian dialects, styles of versification and the intricacies of Italian grammar. But he could, work over, shut his book and be one of the funniest of men, recounting such stories as only his master Lorenzo da Ponte could have admitted to.

SIR COLIN DAVIS conducting the New York Philharmonic Orchestra, Avery Fisher Hall, Lincoln Center, New York

His great love was for Mozart's operas: his dilapidated and heavily annotated scores bore witness to the hours, days and years of his study and experience. *Recitativo secco* was his passion: the abolition of bar lines, a cause in favour of the supremacy of theatrical declamation and the realisation of every possible nuance of Da Ponte's masterly librettos. Students may go to the old Covent Garden recordings to hear how effective his teaching could be.

Of course, Ubaldo's methods could be very upsetting to those who were unwilling to change what they had always done, and he himself would quickly take offence if his authority as an Italian and a musician was challenged. But there were few who quarrelled with him and, certainly, they were the worse off for not listening to him. Those who did learned to love him.

I raise my glass, on behalf of all who remember him with the joy that I do, to *Maestro* Ubaldo Gardini.

Sir Colin Davis

ACKNOWLEDGEMENTS

Preparing an Operatic Role could not have been completed without the support of many people who helped its realisation from the initial idea to publication. I should like to thank them all most sincerely for their co-operation and generosity with their time.

My first thanks go to Ubaldo himself for giving his blessing to the project and then, during interviews both in Italy and Japan, his extraordinary patience and good humour in coping with journalistic questions – rather than the lengthy, erudite discussions about the vast world of opera that he might have preferred.

The person who facilitated our meetings and enabled them to run smoothly was Ubaldo's wife and unofficial manager Reiko Sakuma, an internationally-known television programme co-ordinator. Her involvement both in Poggio Renatico (Ubaldo's home town in Italy) and Tokyo – including researching the Gardini family history, being present at the interviews, and providing materials – was most helpful. Nor could the contributions of those connected with Japanese opera have been made without her help – she became a colleague for whom nothing was too much trouble.

Next are the artists themselves. I owe them all a tremendous debt of gratitude, especially Sir Colin Davis who so very kindly wrote the Foreword. I particularly appreciate how, despite their busy international careers, they and other opera-related personalities made themselves available for interview about their work with Ubaldo. I am also grateful to the artists' efficient agents for providing information and contacts. I could not have managed without their assistance.

Such a book needed extensive background knowledge. I wanted to know more about Ubaldo's life in Italy before his arrival in the UK: about his birthplace Poggio Renatico, his family background, childhood and musical influences; about music in Fascist Italy; about the war and its impact; and, especially, the postwar world of Italian opera where he gained such valuable experience. Since many of his personal documents were lost or destroyed during two traumatic periods of his family's life – first, at the end of World War II when fleeing German soldiers looted homes in his area, and later in 1951 when the nearby flooded river Reno devastated all in its path – extra assistance was required to corroborate Ubaldo's memory of events.

So for this information – and with apologies for research results that do not appear in the book – I wish to thank the following: Dr Luigi Mammolini and the library staff of the Italian Cultural Institute, London, along with Luigi Alva, Daniella Bezzi, Francesca Boesch, *Maestro* Carlo Felice Cillario and his son Lorenzo Cillario, Filippo Ferioli, Claudia Meazzini, Patricia Merlin, Ronaldo Panerai, Dr Francesco Parrino and Romano Silva.

For background on Ubaldo's early career in the UK (Royal Opera House Covent Garden, Glyndebourne Festival Opera, recording companies) and New York (Metropolitan Opera House and the Juilliard School of Music), I spoke to various artists including Richard van Allan, Stafford Dean, Mirella Freni, Peter Gellhorn, Giuseppe Giacomini, Liza Hobbs, Howard T. Howard, Robin Leggate, Jean Mallandaine, Sherrill Milnes, Antonio Petrizzio, Renata Scotto and David Syrus. Others such as Sir Peter Hall, Robert Tear, Jon Vickers, Raymond Leppard and Jesús López-Cobos provided written comments. I am extremely indebted to them all.

I also enlisted the help of staff in various opera house departments and am most grateful to the following for their assistance in confirming details: the archivists of the Royal Opera House Covent Garden (especially, Francesca Franchi and Julia Creed); Glyndebourne Festival Opera (especially, Julia Aries); the Metropolitan Opera House New York and the Juilliard School of Music. Special thanks are also due to the personnel in the press offices at these institutions, particularly, Rita Grudzien at the Royal Opera House.

To check aspects of the book's general contents that required non-musical knowledge, I consulted well-qualified, specialist friends including Katharine Alder, David Banbury, Elizabeth Davies, Jean Kalman, Khac Uyen Nguyen and Gerald Yearsley.

Since I no longer live in Japan, I am thankful to two important figures for their contributions to the Japanese section of Ubaldo's profile. Professor Taikai Takahashi, Head of Opera at Tokyo Geidai (Japan's leading university of the arts) provided an overview of the history of western opera in his country. Mr Yoji Koh, former Executive Director of the Tokyo Nikikai opera company, outlined Ubaldo's achievements as Italian coach and frequent director of productions.

Getting this book to publication involved much general office and administration work, including setting up and maintaining data systems, dealing with correspondence and transcribing taped interviews. For all this I want to thank my three stimulating editorial assistants Lucinda Millward, Miho Sanou and, especially, Kai Hoffman – all with burgeoning arts careers of their own – who helped me at various stages of the work-in-progress.

Over this period I received excellent editorial support from Anne Tennant, Kate Hopkins – and most importantly, Jacky Jackson for final editing and proofreading.

I also wish to pay tribute to SCW's Lee Smith and Claire Hawkes for making the meticulous design process so pleasant – and for their encouragement and patience.

Lastly, I cannot thank enough one of the most important and supportive 'backstage' persons – my husband Tom who, frequently setting his own work aside, unofficially and cheerfully filled many of the functions above.

If I have omitted anyone, I should like to apologise in the Japanese manner with a sincere *gommensai.* To each and everyone who helped me in whatever way, I wish to put on record my warmest thanks.

Marie Myerscough 2008

INTRODUCTION

The legendary Italian language coach, Ubaldo Gardini, belongs to that great tradition of *maestri* who for centuries have travelled abroad to teach their country's opera. After working as an accomplished violinist and occasional coach in his native Italy, often with illustrious singers and conductors, Ubaldo's career continued outside – initially in the UK, then in New York and now in Japan.

His engagement from the late 1960s at the Royal Opera House Covent Garden and Glyndebourne is said to have revolutionised performances of Italian opera in this country both for the stage and for recordings. It is a little-known fact that up to then most people's experience here of this 'foreign' art form consisted of productions sung in English or in less-than-perfect Italian. Ubaldo's crucial role in raising standards is acknowledged not only by the singers and other artists of the time but also by the directors of opera houses and record producers. For this reason many believe that, with his vast musical knowledge, Ubaldo Gardini qualifies as more than a language coach – and is, in fact, a genuine *maestro.*

The artists Ubaldo coached, many of whom are interviewed in this book, constitute a veritable *Who's Who* of international opera. They include Sir Thomas Allen, Dame Janet Baker, Hildegard Behrens, Monserrat Caballé, José Carreras, Ileana Cotrubas, Plácido Domingo, Sir Geraint Evans, Renée Fleming, Dame Kiri Te Kanawa, Benjamin Luxon, Jessye Norman, Luciano Pavarotti, Ruggero Raimondi, Katia Ricciarelli, Renata Scotto, Frederica von Stade, Alan Titus and Ingvar Wixell. Others who have acknowledged their artistic debt to *Maestro* Gardini include conductors Sir Colin Davis, Mark Elder and Eugene Kohn; répétiteurs Katherine Olson and Phillip Thomas; and producer John Copley. Some of the Japanese artists Ubaldo taught have also gone on to international careers, while others are now household names in their native Japan.

It was in Tokyo that I first met Ubaldo and was privileged to see some of his opera productions and interview him for various publications. My journalistic instincts were particularly aroused by one of the often-hidden but crucial elements that go into preparing an opera – namely coaching. Although I had already left Japan and moved back to the UK by the time the idea for this book took hold, I decided to try and interview Ubaldo again in my efforts to learn more about the work of the language coach. Then, I became curious about the responses of performers to his intensive training, and arranged to meet some of those he coached during the various stages of his career. I later converted their replies to my questions into straight narratives which, taken together, combine to create a detailed portrait of Ubaldo and his meticulous way of working.

The interviews are grouped around three full-length chapters – a sketch of Ubaldo's professional career, the general role of coaching in preparing an opera, and some of his guidelines for singing in Italian – complete with his anecdotes and examples of amusing linguistic gaffes when singers mispronounce. Also included is a short article he wrote some 20 years ago for inclusion in a standard British opera guide series, on the background to *Il barbieri di Siviglia*, an opera he has coached many times.

Tackling a project such as this was challenging. First, attempting to convey, in journalistic terms, the intellectualism and artistry necessary for staging a successful opera often felt inadequate and superficial. Trying to encapsulate Ubaldo's vast knowledge into the confines of a book proved even more formidable. Nor could I hope to reproduce his extended answers and explanations, given in an Italianate English so distinctive that it is forever imprinted on the minds of many artists, to be spontaneously revived whenever they get together and reminisce.

Nonetheless, I hope that when those who have worked with Ubaldo read this book, they will be able once more to hear his voice – and perhaps even picture him, somewhat dishevelled-looking in dark suit with tie slightly awry, mopping his ever-perspiring brow or struggling to explain in simple English complicated operatic meanings and concepts from his scribble-covered Italian score. To those readers for whom Ubaldo Gardini is just a name in an opera house programme or who are meeting him for the first time here, I hope they will understand why so many artists feel their careers have been transformed by him.

CONTENTS

PROFILE OF UBALDO GARDINI

ITALY

Setting the Scene

Ubaldo Graziano Giuseppe Luigi Gardini was born on the 18th December 1924 in a small, northern Italian town (population 8,000) not far from the great historic cities of Bologna and Ferrara. This is the *comune* of Poggio Renatico, which sits amid the lush fruit farms and tilled fields of the vast Emilia Romagna plain. Ubaldo's family were originally landowners – whose former wealth is attested to by the impressive Gardini tomb in the local cemetery.

To the foreign eye mainly familiar with medieval or Renaissance Italian towns of narrow streets, irregular topography, villas, hidden gardens and the like, Poggio Renatico is, at first glance, disappointing. Despite its probable Roman origins and a few notable buildings, such as the dominant Bolognese-style Castello Lambertini (now the town hall), and its imposing neighbour, the red-brick church of San Michele Arcangelo, the heart of the town is entirely flat, much of it postwar built. A 'path' of narrow tree-lined streets, flanked by houses and low-rise shops, encloses the large central piazza – which mostly functions nowadays as a car park. Aside from the castle and church, the other striking feature is the large Caffé Centrale which used to serve as a cultural gathering point for the menfolk,

Castello Lambertini which originally belonged to a powerful Bolognese family

including Ubaldo's father, when Ubaldo was young. A shady park with a war memorial and adjacent children's playground complete the scene.

However, a closer look at Poggio Renatico's town centre is more rewarding. On Via Cavour, at the north end of the square and recalling an older architectural style, stand an arcade of low-rise shops and *caffés* next to a large derelict villa set back from its bougainvillea garden. The harmony of these warm buildings is broken sharply by a piece of industrial architecture in cardinal red brick. This three-storey building, with its harsh central tower, was formerly the headquarters of the local Fascist government and today contains municipal offices. (Although Ubaldo was born and grew up in Mussolini's Italy – Bologna was *Il Duce's* birthplace and the centre of fascism – he does not recall any negative impact on his daily life.)

Via Matteotti, adjoining to the south is characterised by detached and shuttered houses in warm colours, with Italianate tiled roofs. The other two streets hold less interest: Via Garibaldi merely separates the piazzas from the *castello* and public garden, while Via Roma consists of a line of 1950s-built small shops and other commercial premises.

A pathway through the park and children's playground leads to Via San Carlo, where Ubaldo Gardini was born and raised and still returns each July and August to escape Tokyo's heat and humidity. This is also the base for his opera summer school – the rich tones of students' singing, interspersed with the quarter-hourly clanging chimes from the castle's clock tower, often the only sounds to break the normal daytime quiet.

While most of Poggio Renatico's adult population these days commute by train and car to nearby Bologna and Ferrara, during Ubaldo's childhood few people worked outside what was then a village. The majority were local farmers and rural labourers, while others were employed in small businesses. Gardini's father, Angelo, a mechanical engineer ran one such firm, an engineering works, Officina Garage Gardini, established in 1920. Here on Via San Carlo where Ubaldo's brother, Luigi (who took over the business), his wife and children still live and next to the house that hosts the summer school, Angelo and a handful of mechanics made and repaired metal machinery, tools and implements for other companies, farms and domestic use. (Ubaldo's family home stood next to the workshop.)

Ubaldo, aged ten with his younger brother, Luigi

While the *comune* enjoyed a modest cultural life with local concerts in the *castello* or a small theatre, along with occasional opera performances by travelling companies, it was largely from his extended family that Ubaldo inherited his interest in music and the arts. Influential relatives (who lived above the repairshop) were his grandparents, especially grandmother Attilia, with literary, musical and mathematical talents, and her daughter Aunt Bianca, 'a great artist who also taught me how to paint,' he says.

However, it is his father, Angelo, whose interests extended well beyond engineering, to whom Ubaldo feels most indebted. A self-taught violinist and widely read, Angelo was fascinated by the intellectual aspects of music as well as science and mathematics. An inventor of machines, he was also a grandmaster of chess and a devotee of poetry, able to recite Dante's *La divina commedia* by heart. Ubaldo is proud of his father whom he considered to be 'a learned man with one of the greatest minds I've ever come across'.

Born the eldest of three sons, one of whom died in infancy, Ubaldo paints a picture of his home with plentiful books and music. Angelo was also a mandolin player in an amateur ensemble that often rehearsed in the family's living quarters. They would also listen to radio broadcasts of the best of the popular new operas, including those by Pietro Mascagni and Riccardo Zandonai.

When he was just five, Ubaldo started learning the violin from a local teacher who taught a children's class in one of the rooms in the *castello*. His talent soon revealed itself and he recalls 'appearances' in the town when he was billed as a child star. During his formal education at the *scuola elementari* in Poggio and *scuola secondari* in nearby Ferrara, he continued taking lessons with various private teachers. The most important *maestri*, including Paganini expert, Bruto Michelini, were at this city's Liceo Musicale Frescobaldi – back then a music high school, and now a music conservatoire. Ubaldo's violin studies culminated in the *liceo's* highest award, the final diploma, which, following the disruptions caused by World War II, was only presented in 1949.

World War II

Italy entered the war in the autumn of 1940 but did not experience much fighting on home soil until the Allied invasion of July 1943 – after which the situation suddenly changed, plunging the country, especially the north, into destruction and death on an unprecedented scale. Mussolini was overthrown and the Fascist regime collapsed. The subsequent surrender of the new Royalist government to the Allies resulted in the disintegration of the army, and deserting soldiers changing sides to fight against the Nazis – with the Allies and/or the Partisan Resistance.

Italy, formerly on the side of Germany, now became its enemy. Hitler retaliated by rushing in divisions of his forces to occupy most of the country, which, with two opposing armies locked in conflict, was transformed into a battleground that claimed hundreds of thousands of lives.

The next two years were characterised by fierce combat in which nearly every piece of terrain had to be fought over, and cities were bombed. After the June 1944 liberation of Rome, the Allies' northerly push to free the rest of the country created a situation verging on civil war. The fighting in Emilia Romagna was the most prolonged, with Bologna and Ferrara among the last Italian cities to be liberated – just weeks before Germany officially surrendered on 2nd May 1945.

However, the fortunate Ubaldo avoided active service and the ravages of war – initially by being a student at the (now-defunct) Guglielmo Marconi Technical Institute in Bologna and later, when it caught up with him, by being given a non-combative role in the equivalent of an entertainment corps. Here he organised instrumentalists and singers to provide regular *serata della canzone* evenings of popular song, mainly for civilians in the Ferrara area.

This experience of leading a group of musicians reinforced a dream Ubaldo had secretly harboured – of becoming an orchestral conductor. When the war ended he attempted to pursue that career – though not by the conventional route. 'I thought, why should I go to a conservatoire, with its regimented curriculum. I wanted to be free, to learn more than they teach you in those places. When you go to great violinists for lessons, they don't keep you down and force you to follow their syllabus. They teach you what you want to learn. Paganini never went to a conservatoire,' he concludes triumphantly. Instead, Ubaldo set his sights on cultured Florence, where he felt he could learn whatever he wanted. He moved there in 1946.

Florence

Apart from minor bomb damage by the Allies – including to the Teatro Comunale opera house – Florence was largely spared the massive destruction inflicted on other Italian cities. Thus, by the time Ubaldo arrived, it was well on its way to recovery. He did not take long to make contacts with other musicians, who not only provided him with playing opportunities but also introduced him to teachers for occasional lessons in various aspects of Italian culture, such as Florentine Italian, *arte dramatica*, poetry and art history. These were combined with a large element of self-education.

This period in postwar Italy was a golden age for Ubaldo. He benefited from a situation whereby beneath a superficial stranglehold of bureaucracy and strong labour unions, in reality the day-to-day organisation of the opera houses was comparatively loose and relaxed. For instance, conductors and other established musicians could draft in friends to swell orchestral numbers or sit in on rehearsals. The distinguished conductor, *Maestro* Carlo Felice Cillario, concurs and explains that the patronage enjoyed by artists and musicians under Mussolini continued after the war. 'We were privileged by the system,' he says, 'the opportunity to make [cultural] propaganda for music and by music.'

This casual environment offered Ubaldo unique opportunities to 'learn on the job'. A combination of deputising and session playing in opera orchestras (most significantly, under Vittorio Gui in Florence, and further afield at La Scala Milan, under Tullio Serafin), as well as attending rehearsals of great artists such as Renata Tebaldi and Tito Gobbi with conductors including Vittorio De Sabata, provided him with valuable training.

In Florence especially, Ubaldo was often asked to assist as an extra coach with the *preparazione* of singers who ranged from students to budding professionals – all of which infused him with a passion for the human voice that would later alter the course of his life. Among the rising stars, the most notable was the 25-year-old Maria Callas, who made her debut as Violetta in the 1951 production of *La Traviata* at the Teatro Comunale under Serafin. All this experience is a source of great satisfaction to Ubaldo. 'I think I learned so much more doing things that way. By the time I was thirty, I probably knew most of the well-known opera scores and libretti,' he says.

However, this occasional work did not pay well and the versatile Ubaldo, now in his late-twenties, was fortunate to get a job in a local dance band performing on saxophone and clarinet, which he had taught himself. American dance music, forbidden under Mussolini, was now the rage.

An equally lucrative engagement was playing the violin in one of the city's renowned *caffés*. Florence at this time was once again attracting tourists and its *caffé concerti* (coffee houses with chamber orchestras providing live music) offered good opportunities to capable musicians. Ubaldo played in the oldest and most famous of them all, Caffé Paszkowski in the Piazza de la Republica.

Top: Ubaldo enjoys a solo spot with the *caffé concerto* orchestra
Above: Ubaldo with other musicians of the versatile ensemble

A typical *caffé concerto* in the shadow of Brunelleschi's *duomo*, Florence

'We were about twelve people in all,' he recalls, 'three violins, viola, cello, double bass, clarinet and piano, plus singers. Along with popular music, we also played arias from the operas. The *caffé concerto* was secure work.' Ubaldo also makes the point that in terms of continental European culture, he is not the only classical musician to earn money this way: 'Dvorák did it. Even Toscanini loved to conduct these little bands.'

Performing at this *caffé* was to provide a turning point in Ubaldo Gardini's life. One day in 1952 among its tourist clientele was a famous Australian mezzo-soprano, Sylvia Fisher. At that time Covent Garden's leading dramatic soprano, especially renowned for her Wagnerian roles, she often performed in Italy. Her travelling companion, Carmen d'Ossa, a film-maker, relates how music brought Ubaldo and Fisher together. 'At first, Sylvia didn't admit that she was a singer. But while Ubaldo showed us round Florence, impressing us with his knowledge of painting, architecture – and of music – finally she let it out. He asked her if she'd ever sung with De Sabata and other famous Italian conductors. She said yes, she had. So then, he was awfully thrilled. Later that year she was going to sing Sieglinde in Rome and he came down to her first night.'

THE ROYAL OPERA HOUSE COVENT GARDEN, GLYNDEBOURNE FESTIVAL OPERA, RECORDINGS

Ubaldo's arrival in London for another of Sylvia's debuts – as Isolde at the Royal Opera House Covent Garden under Sir George Barbirolli in January 1953 – was the start of his new life in Britain. The violinist infatuated with the human voice was now in love with an international diva. They married early in 1954. His violin playing ended but a new career beckoned as an Italian coach for opera – albeit after a slow start.

Despite being well equipped for a musical career in England at a time when a number of foreign *émigrés* (mainly refugees from Nazism) were in leading positions in the arts, it took Ubaldo almost a decade to become established. Occasional one-off jobs back in Italy to coach on recordings, including most notably a La Scala *L'elisir d'amore* conducted by Tullio Serafin with Luigi Alva and Rolando Panerai, did help to keep his hand in. (Both singers attest to his skill as a *preparatore.*) Finally, informal requests for private lessons by opera singers and other professionals, along with occasional work at the London Opera Centre, led to his being offered a position at the Royal Opera House Covent Garden in 1966, as Italian coach – and 'on a casual basis'.

A contract for Glyndebourne's summer seasons swiftly followed. In 1971 his status at the Royal Opera House was upgraded to permanent member of the music staff. His work there was supplemented by regular engagements as language coach for Europe's main recording companies, most notably Philips. When in 1981 he moved to the Metropolitan Opera House New York he remained attached to Covent Garden on short-term contracts for another two years. During this time Ubaldo Gardini was the UK's most sought-after Italian opera coach.

Sir John Tooley, then general director of the Royal Opera House, sums up that period as fortunate. 'There was a stability that had been built up under artistic directors Erich Kleiber, Rafael Kubelík and Sir Georg Solti,' he explains. He describes Ubaldo as a lynchpin of the Colin Davis era that followed (1971–85), and essential to the musical aims of the House. He cites several talents – how he got singers to understand the meaning and dramatic points of the music, to build credible characters, and sing more naturally. His work on the recitative was particularly significant. In fact, Sir John says, 'after the [previous] conventional approach, it was amazing to discover from Ubaldo's achievements with the language how he could transform the singing into something that was theatrical, highly musical and alive. It really grabbed you'.

Of all the operas on which Ubaldo worked at the Royal Opera House, those with which he is most associated are three acclaimed Mozart productions of the Davis era. *Le Nozze di Figaro* (December 1971) starred Geraint Evans as Figaro and Reri Grist as Susanna – but was probably most notable for Dame Kiri Te Kanawa's debut as the Countess Almaviva. (Ubaldo was closely involved in her year-long prepara-

Artistic Director Colin Davis and Ubaldo at the Royal Opera House Covent Garden

Monserrat Caballé as Tosca with Peter Glossop as Scarpia, a Royal Opera House production coached by Ubaldo and conducted by Colin Davis

tion for this role in which she was such a success.) This was followed by *Don Giovanni* (April 1973), with Peter Glossop in the lead, Gwyneth Jones as Donna Anna and Geraint Evans as Leporello. The third was *Così fan tutte* (January 1981), with Stuart Burrows as Ferrando, Thomas Allen as Guglielmo, Agnes Baltsa as Dorabella and Kiri Te Kanawa as Fiordiligi.

Meanwhile, at Glyndebourne where Ubaldo worked from 1967 until 1975, Chairman Sir George Christie comments how Ubaldo came at the right time, just when the opera company was going through a bad patch. 'However, the problem was mended with [producer] Peter Hall and [conductor] John Pritchard' he says.

Sir John Pritchard has written how Ubaldo 'was not only a language coach... but a musician and operatic expert with knowledge covering a wide repertory.' Sir Peter Hall, producer during that period of such operas as *La Calisto, Il ritorni d'Ulisse in patria, Le Nozze di Figaro, Don Giovanni* and *Così fan tutte* says how he enjoyed working with Ubaldo, especially for the fact that 'he had as much respect for the drama as he did for the music.'

Looking back, Sir George Christie explains how Ubaldo brought new insights to productions and was regarded as indispensable among conductors and music staff. From the late Moran Caplat, General Administrator, the redoubtable Jani Strasser, Head of Music, and his successor, Martin Isepp, to conductors Raymond Leppard and Jesús López-Cobos – Glyndebourne's music *supremos* all pay tribute to Ubaldo's achievements, especially his illumination of textual subtleties and the excellent training he provided in Italian pronunciation.

To many of those with whom Ubaldo worked he gave the impression of regarding himself as the official custodian of the Italian language, seeming to take linguistic errors as a personal affront. Stories are legion of how a nervous young novice's faulty *buon giorno* on their first meeting would be turned into an entire coaching session devoted to getting the Italian 'good morning' right. But the end result was a whole generation – the first – of talented young British singers starting out their careers with the confidence, strength and style to give acclaimed performances, not just in the UK but in major opera houses around the world.

The huge affection and respect felt by the company at Glyndebourne, and their sense of loss when Ubaldo left in 1975, are summed up by Sir George Christie: 'When he decided not to return to Glyndebourne we were extremely sorry. I knew him not only as a member of the company but also as a friend.'

Recordings

From the late 1960s to the early 1980s, during the period generally regarded as the golden age of quality recordings, and in a natural extension of his work for the stage, Ubaldo was engaged as the Italian coach for a number of recording companies. With Philips in particular, he was an integral part of the music team and is said to have left his mark on every set of operatic LPs with which he was involved. Most notable among those conducted by Sir Colin Davis and produced by the renowned Erik Smith are: *Le Nozze di Figaro, Don Giovanni, Così fan tutte, Tosca, La clemenza di Tito, Un ballo in maschera, La Bohème* and *Il Trovatore*. Ubaldo's association with Decca, RCA, EMI and other labels saw him working on a range of recordings led by other distinguished conductors, such as Lamberto Gardelli, Sir Neville Marriner, James Levine, Lorin Maazel, Richard Bonynge and Raymond Leppard. The soloists, some of whom he also prepared for their individual contracts, were the leading international singers of their generation.

Artists and music staff – especially at Philips – recall Ubaldo at these recording sessions, attentively following the score, guiding the singers, and then in the control room listening to the 'takes'. His broad musical knowledge, including erudite references to the composers' intentions culled from their writings, along with personal recollections of historic productions conducted by such 'greats' as Toscanini, De Sabata and Serafin, made him a respected authority. Also remembered is the book he carried round with him, the García *Treatise on Singing*, which he would consult in response to queries or 'quote selectively to back up his own theories', according to producer Erik Smith.

In addition to his linguistic and literary expertise, Ubaldo was influential in two other musical areas. The first was stylistic – and about which he was passionate – namely, the *appoggiatura* decoration. David Cairns, at the time in Philips Academic and Research department, explains that hitherto the British tradition was to sing a very straight melodic line with little ornamentation. Ubaldo, however, believed that if you did not do the *appoggiatura* the music would not be sung in the Italian way – that is, says Cairns, 'with a mellifluous delivery of the text'. He cites a 1968 recording of *Idomeneo* where Ubaldo's influence is audible on every track. 'I don't believe any other Colin Davis recording has so many *appoggiaturas*,' he exclaims.

However, once more it was Ubaldo's contribution to the recitatives that is particularly noteworthy. They, too, had a different history and were often meaninglessly rattled off, according to Erik Smith.

But 'now Ubaldo made them sound like spoken Italian'. To help the singers achieve this naturalness, he would conduct them 'with precision and finesse,' Smith says, adding, 'you could see how he really loved conducting'.

When verbal explanations failed and singers could not understand what he was trying to teach, Ubaldo's solution, usually signalled by the phrase '*per esempio*,' (here meaning, 'copy me'), was to sing the phrase for them to imitate. This simple method resulted in those with a good ear – even when they did not understand what they were singing – being able to sound authentically Italian. Many musicians say how when they listen to recordings of that period, those that Ubaldo worked on are immediately recognisable.

Ubaldo's other talents did not go unappreciated – especially as a witty raconteur. David Cairns comments how after tense recording sessions it was very important to relax. 'Ubaldo refreshed us, entertaining us with his fund of stories in Italianate English.' Nor was Ubaldo always just the voice behind the scenes. On one *La Traviata* recording he

Ubaldo with conductor James Levine after a recording

sings the minor role of Giuseppe – in the company of Dame Joan Sutherland and Luciano Pavarotti, no less.

Legendary, then, throughout the opera world in Britain, and with an international reputation from the many conductors and artists with whom he worked, in 1981 Ubaldo Gardini accepted a tempting offer to move to the Metropolitan Opera House New York. He left alone, his marriage to Sylvia Fisher dissolved and his long-term relationship with Eva Kondra (a costume maker at Glyndebourne by whom he had three children) ended. His less-than-perfect domestic life had occasionally impinged on his professional commitments, but to no great extent. As a result, most artists at Covent Garden were devastated by Ubaldo's departure and wondered how they could ever manage without him.

[Now settled adults, leading successful, creative careers, Ubaldo's sons and daughter have since been re-united with him. Angelo, an IT manager, and Zsuzsanna, a fashion textile designer, both live in the UK; while Michael, a photographer, is based in the United States.]

THE METROPOLITAN OPERA HOUSE NEW YORK

Between 1981 and 1984 Ubaldo was rostered at the Met as Italian language coach and prompter, each season working on a range of operas with a variety of singers. He also taught at the neighbouring prestigious Juilliard School of Music. However, his sojourn in New York did not live up to expectations and he encountered professional difficulties for the first time in his career. One reason may have been the Met's gigantic size and turnover 'a factory churning out operas at a fast rate,' according to Artistic Administrator, Jonathan Friend. But whatever the specifics, Ubaldo's personality and way of working did not sit well with many artists in that vast institution.

Nonetheless, he did have several notable supporters. Italian tenor, Giuseppe Giacomini, although not personally coached by him, remarks on the *maestro's* great knowledge of opera and his meticulousness. 'From what I observed and his remarks to me after a performance, I could see that he was looking at the small things, details that were important. Coaches like Ubaldo are good for young singers starting their careers,' he says. In fact, Ubaldo's work with emerging talents such as soprano Renée Fleming and *répétiteur* Katherine Olson, both interviewed for this book, illustrates this very well.

Fabrizio Melano, an established theatre designer and now a freelance director, also worked quite closely with him – as a producer – and assesses his strength as the ability to force people to look at things differently, that is, 'unsettling one's complacency'. He recalls his production of *Trittico*, and the challenge Ubaldo's knowledge and sense of the Italian style presented. Asked to suggest what went wrong at the Met, one factor he suggests is Ubaldo's perfectionism, 'he wasn't able to do the in-depth work he wanted'.

JAPAN

Tokyo Geidai University of the Arts

In 1984, when Ubaldo was sixty, he was invited to apply for a job that would take him to the other side of the world – to Japan, where he later married Reiko, his second wife. He was appointed as Visiting Professor of Italian opera at Japan's most prestigious arts university, Tokyo Geijutsu Daigaku (Tokyo Geidai, for short).This was the first time an Italian with international experience and the ambition to forge links between Japanese singers and the opera world overseas had held such a position. Professor Taikai Takahashi, head of the opera department at the time and himself a professional singer, nostalgically recalls the importance of Ubaldo's appointment as 'significant for Japan as the arrival of the Black Ships' – a reference to the opening up of the country at the end of the 19th century, signaled by the landing of the US Fleet under Commander Matthew Perry.

Despite some difficulties, Ubaldo was able to broaden his career in Japan with new creative opportunities that might not have been available had he stayed in the West. During his twenty years at Geidai, Gardini-*sensei* (a Japanese honorific title meaning teacher/professor) has been responsible for several remarkable productions, starting with *Idomeneo* in his first year and later, *Così fan tutte*, *La clemenza di Tito*, *Le Nozze di Figaro* and *Il barbiere di*

Siviglia. Professor Takahashi says of that first *Idomeneo* how 'it was a surprise to discover that we could stage an opera of such a high standard. The libretto, drama and music all came together in a way we hadn't seen before. We felt that Geidai was on the threshold of something new'.

Gardini-*sensei* was equally impressed with the talent of his students, who were mainly postgraduates. However, he had to work hard to initiate them into the conventions of Italian opera. When Japan became westernised at the end of the 19th century the country's first music teachers were from Germany. Consequently, that country's traditions have dominated Japanese musical education ever since. Overcoming this legacy presented *Sensei* with a challenge. Students (and some staff), used to the detail and complexity of the German style, found it difficult to adapt to the simpler structure and freer (that is, less prescriptive) scores of its Italian rival. The difficulty of subsuming their Japanese-ness to act out Western roles in an individual and realistic manner was compounded by problems with the Italian language and culture. The singing, too, was in a heavy, Germanic style. 'Students were singing my operas like a concert performance,' Gardini complains. He had one shorthand signal to end the stiffness and excessive emoting. '*Tedesco, tedesco*' ('That's the German way'), he would shout.

Nevertheless, many committed students, some of whom appear in this book, did survive the relentless 'Gardini method' and went on to achieve success in Japan. Sadly, though, their prospects for an international career are limited – the only available opportunities for talented singers lie generally within the domestic scene. This is mainly because Japan has no national opera company to serve as a training ground and route to an international career. Another difficulty is the gulf between this strictly Japanese world and that of foreign touring companies, in effect separating opera audiences into two mutually exclusive groups – those who attend only star-studded productions by the Met, Vienna State Opera and others, and those loyal to the domestic companies.

Ubaldo made several attempts to bridge this gap by creating relationships with opera companies outside Japan. The most notable, in spring 1989, was an international workshop on the Brescia edition of *Madama Butterfly* for both Japanese students at Tokyo Geidai and Americans from the San Francisco Opera Center. (Ubaldo regards the Brescia version as the only authentic edition.) The guest artist was soprano Akiko Nakajima from Opera Australia. The aim was to create the ideal production with – as far as possible – Japanese playing the Japanese roles and Americans playing Pinkerton, Kate and the Consul, Sharpless. But in true cross-cultural spirit – and thinking ahead to possible future careers – *Maestro* also had the singers swap roles.

This project, produced by Ubaldo's wife Reiko and typifying Japanese all-out effort and co-operation, was unprecedented in both scale and ambition. A large 'cast' was involved – including singers, pianists, orchestra, creative and technical teams, along with a legion of behind-the-scenes volunteers. A three-week programme of workshops and rehearsals culminated in performances at Tokyo Geidai and out-of-town venues, ending appropriately in another well-known Japanese port city – not Nagasaki, the original setting for *Madama Butterfly* – but Yokohama, location of the prestigious university, Keio.

An accompanying series of cultural activities was organised to provide the students with information about the opera's background. Visits to places as diverse as shrines and temples, the tomb of Japan's best-known Butterfly (soprano Tamaka Miuri who died in 1946), even a US military base, were supplemented by lectures on such themes as the history of the opera and its place in the context of 19th century Italy, the USA and Japan. One of the great masters of Japanese dance, Kikushiro Onoe, teacher to *kabuki* actors, gave movement classes – equally necessary for today's young Japanese.

Despite the talent of the 'home' students, now nearly two decades later it is the San Francisco alumni (Patricia Racette, Craig Estep, LeRoy Villanueva and Reveka Mavrovitis) who have gone on to success in both the USA and overseas. Of the Japanese, while mezzo-soprano Akemi Sakamoto is now a household name in Japan, only the pianist Sumiko Tokushima has been engaged to work abroad – as a *répétiteur* at the Tirol Landestheater Innsbruck.

Scenes from the 1989 *Madama Butterfly* international workshop, with Patricia Racette in the title role. Top: with Akemi Sakamoto as Suzuki. Above: with students of the Enomoto Singing School

Scene from a masterclass at Tokyo Geidai on *Otello*, directed by Plácido Domingo (seated at table far left)

Other important Ubaldo innovations in Japan – and part of the normal syllabus in the world's major conservatoires to prepare students for a performing career – were master classes and lectures by internationally known singers. In these he involved such former 'protégés' as Frederica von Stade, Donald McIntyre, John Dobson, Plácido Domingo, Alan Titus, Sherrill Milnes and Ruggero Raimondi. Sadly, once Gardini-*sensei* retired, the scheme ended.

Japanese Opera Companies – Tokyo Nikikai

Besides his great achievements at Geidai, other opportunities for *Maestro* Gardini (as he's also known in Japan) to further develop his own career came through working with Japan's domestic opera companies – often as director and designer. The ensemble with which he has been most associated is the highly regarded Nikikai. Over the years, in addition to language coaching and other creative roles, Ubaldo has also acted as artistic adviser to the conductor and director. He is best known for productions including *L'elisir d'amore, Tosca, Madama Butterfly, Rigoletto, La Bohème, Simon Boccanegra, L'incoronazione di Poppea, Trittico* and *Le Nozze di Figaro* – with some being staged at Tokyo's New National Theatre.

Ubaldo brought a fresh approach to these Nikikai operas, according to former executive director, Joji Koh. Referring to the legacy of the German tradition, for example, he acknowledges how it left the company at a disadvantage in their interpretation of Italian opera, how their insecurity made them rely heavily on the conductor, and how they would often overplay the slapstick or farcical elements in Mozart.

Matters were remedied by *Maestro's* almost fanatical way of working. His familiarity with the libretto produced a new realisation of its subtleties, while his insistence on total accuracy in both music and diction ('one hour to coach a bar!'), guaranteed that his 'teachings seeped into the cast'. His emphasis on the importance of the upbeat drew from both the singers and orchestra 'a wonderful *legato*,' concludes Mr Koh.

Ubaldo is equally complimentary about the talents of Japanese singers. He is particularly impressed by their diligence, high level of musical education and accommodationg attitude. His recurrent hope is that Japan 'will soon turn the corner and start to produce more international artists'. But the first step is to have a reputation at home – as many of Nikikai's singers do. In addition to the previously mentioned Akemi Sakamoto, others who are household names in Japan include Yasuhiko Idame (tenor), Hiroshi Kuroda and Satoru Aoto (baritones), along with Mami Koshigoe and Tomoko Shimazaki (sopranos).

The behind-the-scenes personnel also draw *Maestro* Gardini's admiration. 'The set, lighting and costume designers are as highly skilled as any professionals abroad,' he asserts. 'I have directed *Idomeneo* and *Figaro* in the public theatres in Tokyo and each time the creative team and backstage staff have resolved seemingly impossible situations with near-miraculous results.' He attributes it to a combination of the Japanese aesthetic sense, the teamwork and concept of '*ganbarimasho*', meaning 'let's make a supreme effort'.

Private Teaching

Ubaldo continues to give private lessons to both professional and amateur singers at the typical Japanese home he shares with his wife in a small, quiet suburb near Shinjuku in northwest Tokyo. A ten-minute walk from the local train station through a narrow shopping street takes students (usually with accompanists in tow) to a high-walled house fronted by a small garden, complete with the traditional Japanese carp pond and cherry tree. Then up some steps to the front door, after which it is shoes off and slippers on in the *genkan* hall. Opposite the kitchen a sliding door leads to Ubaldo's cluttered music room with its grand piano, music stands, several violins and mandolins, stacks of books on every aspect of opera production, and piles of scores.

A sofa and easy chairs surround a large, low table that is usually covered in more volumes, leaving just enough room for the obligatory green tea or coffee that will precede the lesson. When not teaching this is where Ubaldo Gardini sits, constantly occupied in reading from his vast library or planning his next big project. Behind him is a 'backdrop' of own-design posters from his various Japanese productions – and his paintings.

Inspired by his engineer father – and the great Leonardo da Vinci, no less – the creative Ubaldo is also a compulsive inventor of small gadgets which are intended to be used as teaching aids. They include a Tibetan *mandala*-like drawing to demonstrate the Italian vowel system, a model of a diaphragm to represent the physiological aspects of breathing, a metronome with lights, and an acoustic machine to show how overtones are made. He is particularly proud of a wind-up watch that goes anti-clockwise – copied from that of his left-handed hero, Leonardo.

This then is the setting for the many Japanese singers and musicians who are privileged to enjoy Gardini-*sensei's* private coaching. Some have made it to the international stage. Soprano Akiko Nakajima, previously at Opera Australia (Sydney Opera House), is currently living in Vienna and performs in European opera houses and concert halls. Conductor Kazushi Ono is musical director of Théâtre de la Monnaie Opera House Brussels.

Until recently, in order to maintain his contact with the European opera world Ubaldo has also accepted invitations to work outside Japan on specific projects such as coaching, master classes, and to adjudicate music competitions. Singers at the National Opera Company of Korea in Seoul, the Vienna Volksoper and Staatsoper, and in international competitions in Denmark and Italy, have all benefited from his expertise.

Retirement – and a New Career

In 2004, aged eighty, Ubaldo retired after twenty years' service at Tokyo Geidai – a retirement age, until recently, not uncommon in Japan. He immediately took up a new, part-time post at another institution, Seitoku University, where once a week he lectures and coaches opera to both undergraduates and teachers of the Master's course. Here, he continues to enjoy the Japanese *sensei* privileges of respectful students meeting him, carrying his bags, and escorting him around the campus.

After his long sojourn in Japan, *Maestro* Gardini is now acknowledged there as a leading authority on Italian opera. Hence, he enjoys something of a freelance career, which includes giving master classes in music conservatoires along with lectures elsewhere to groups of knowledgeable adult opera fans. Aware of his uniqueness as their only authentic link to the rich traditions of Italian opera, Japanese *aficionados* flock to hear him speak about it and recount the many anecdotes from his long, international career.

A highlight of *Maestro's* work in Japan took place in September 2007 when he designed and directed a triumphant *Le Nozze di Figaro* to mark the centenary of Tokyo Music College. With the main roles taken by graduates and staff, this important production was staged at the city's main opera venue, Tokyo Bunka Kaikan in Ueno – usually reserved for world-class opera companies from abroad. The assistant director was Takahiro Itoh while Junichi Nakagami, slowly garnering an international reputation, conducted the orchestra. The artistic team consisted of Ubaldo's regular collaborators – Yasuo Okuhata, lighting; Sonoko Watanabe, costumes; and Masahiko Onita as stage manager.

Scene from *Le Nozze di Figaro* student production for the centenary of Tokyo Music College, September 2007

Keizo Takahashi, who played the title role, and is currently professor of Italian opera at the college and executive director of the production, explained beforehand why they chose Gardini: 'The dean, vice-dean and other teaching staff are aware what a great miracle he accomplished with our production of *Don Giovanni* five years ago. We all know about the breadth of his knowledge of Italian opera and his consolidated skills based on his worldwide experience – especially in Mozart. It is extremely difficult to find someone like him. We are absolutely convinced that only with *Maestro* Gardini's direction could we accomplish such a challenging production. We also know that working with him is the best way to stage an opera worthy of our centenary.'

This confidence was justified in a triumphant, sell-out production – provoking the normally restrained Japanese audience into exuberant applause and 'bravos' when the curtain went down. Mr Takahashi enthuses how Ubaldo's artistic concept and direction, his love for all the elements of the opera – especially the drama and the emotional basis of the text – and his encouragement of the student cast – resulted in a dynamic production. As a teacher himself, Takahashi comments, 'it was wonderful to see how these young singers blossomed under *Maestro's* energetic, passionate and authoritative direction'.

MEET THE ARTISTS

Biographies & Interviews Part One

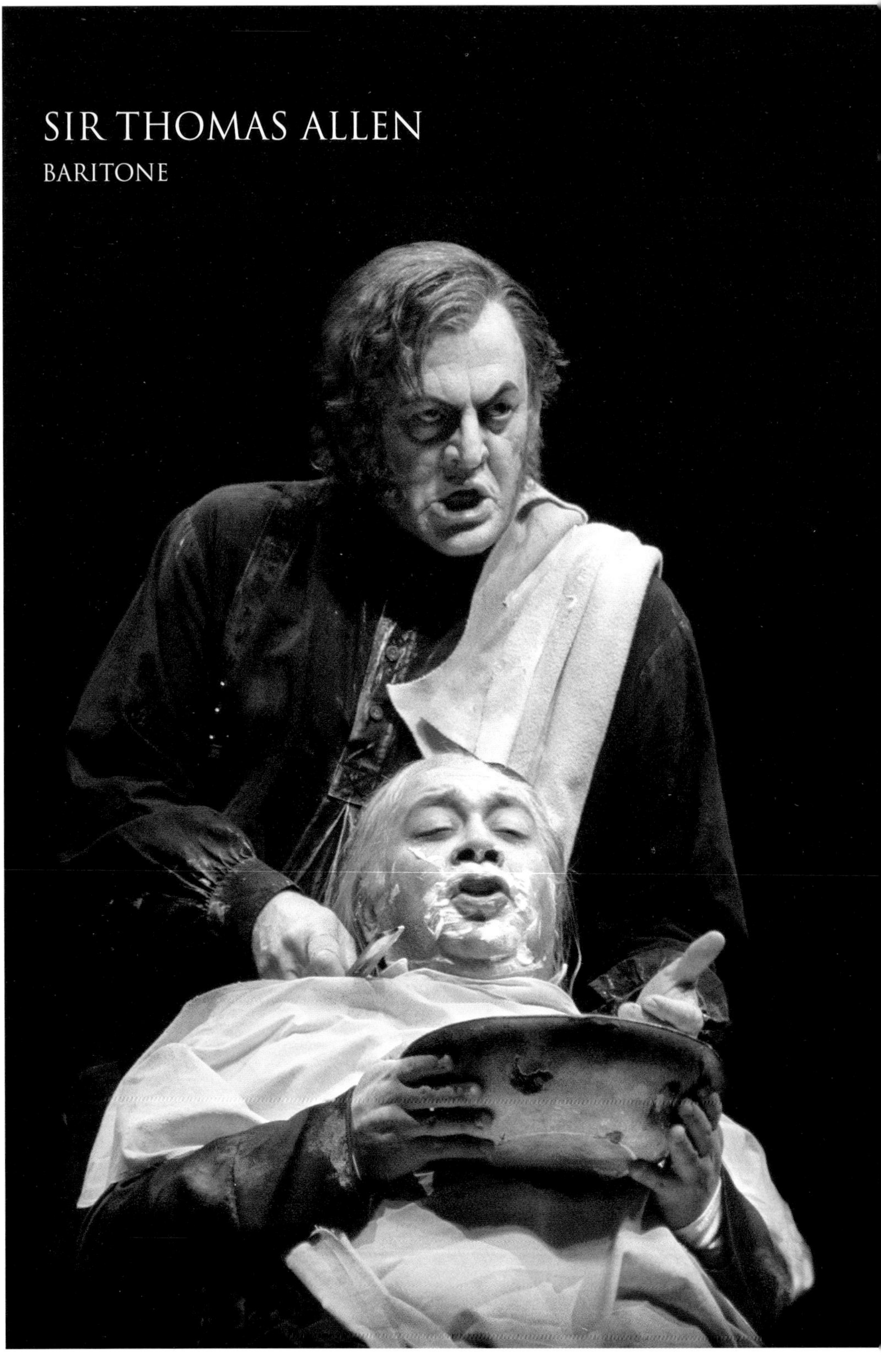

…as the Demon Barber, *Sweeney Todd*, Royal Opera House Covent Garden

Sir Thomas Allen is an established star of the world's great opera houses. In 2006, he celebrated the anniversaries of two major debuts: his thirty-fifth at the Royal Opera House Covent Garden, and his twenty-fifth at the Metropolitan Opera House New York.

He has been particularly acclaimed for his performances of Billy Budd, Pelléas, Eugene Onegin, Ulisse and Beckmesser, as well as the great Mozart roles: Count Almaviva, Don Alfonso, Papageno and Don Giovanni.

Equally renowned on the concert platform, Thomas Allen frequently appears in recital in the United Kingdom, Europe, Australia and the United States. He has sung with the world's leading orchestras and conductors. Most of his repertoire has been recorded with such distinguished conductors as Solti, Levine, Marriner, Haitink, Rattle, Sawallisch and Muti.

His first book, *Foreign Parts – A Singer's Journal*, was published in 1993. He made triumphant directing debuts with *Albert Herring* at London's Royal College of Music and in 2006 with *Le Nozze di Figaro* for Arizona Opera. His many honours include the title of Bayerischer Kammersänger awarded by the Bayerische Staatsoper Munich. He is also Prince Consort Professor of the Royal College of Music, holds the Hambro Visiting Professorship of Opera Studies at Oxford University, and is a fellow of the University of Sunderland.

Sir Thomas Allen was created a Commander of the British Empire (CBE) in 1989 and a Knight Bachelor in 1999.

Ubaldo Gardini coached Sir Thomas in the following roles at the Royal Opera House Covent Garden: Silvio (I pagliacci), *Count Almaviva* (Le Nozze di Figaro), *Guglielmo* (Così fan tutte), *Marcello* (La Bohème) *and Sharpless* (Madama Butterfly); *and for recordings including* Don Giovanni, Le Nozze di Figaro *and* Il barbiere di Siviglia.

'Although I first met Ubaldo in 1969 when I was in the chorus at Glyndebourne, I didn't really get to know him until our work together at the Royal Opera House. I came there from a company in Wales that sang, at that time anyhow, everything in English translation. So with hardly any knowledge of Italian, my arrival at Covent Garden was slightly in fear and trepidation. I knew some French and German – and being a Geordie, the latter came relatively easily. But, Italian, on the other hand, in the sounds that it made, was a land far away.

'I think the first role we worked on was the Count in *Figaro* – I was the understudy. I remember the first recitative, which is "Susanna, tu mi sembri agitate, e confusa." And I started off by saying "Susanna, tu mi semb..." "No." "Susanna, tu mi se..." "No." Well, after half an hour, I hadn't even got the first sentence out, and we were almost at daggers drawn. But, since I'm patient and tolerant and like getting things right, I stuck with it, and it paid off. When I look at my scores now, they're full of the markings from Ubaldo's lessons.

'He would never let you go home, digest an idea overnight and come back the following morning. He wanted perfection to happen there and then, and if it didn't you had to endure endless drilling until you achieved it. He could be irritating but he got results.

'Conveying authentic Italian-ness was important to Ubaldo, that is, to hear his language properly pronounced. Many of the sound colours on my palette today have their origin in what I learned from him. He may not have seen me through these latter years, but he laid down the principles on which I've always worked – and try to instill in today's young singers.

'I went to Italy early on in my career to give concerts and to travel. It made me aware of a different culture which I knew existed but needed to be there to experience. I think in a way Ubaldo, with his pride in being Italian, was our connection to that country.

'His literary background made it all the more fascinating. I remember him urging Erik Smith at Philips Records to read Metastasio [a 17th-century Italian poet and great opera librettist]. It became clear we were dealing with someone whose approach was derived from an intellectual point of view. To be a successful singer is not only a question of having a good voice; it also requires infinite curiosity about the wider aspects of one's subject, such as the literature, the painting, the history. Just being in a conversation where Metastasio's name was dropped made me realise the range of that study.

'Ubaldo is a typically Latin, emotional man. I could imagine him crying at a beautiful piece of Italian music. His character imprinted itself on one's mind – along with the ever-present handkerchief, the pocket full of pencils of different colours, and the briefcase bursting at the seams with extraordinarily-marked scores.'

...in the title role, *Mary Stuart*, English National Opera

Dame Janet Baker was an internationally acclaimed singer for over thirty years. In the United Kingdom, she was made a CBE in 1970, a DBE in 1979 and a Companion of Honour in 1994. She is also the recipient of numerous international awards, most notably, Commander of the French Order of Arts and Letters.

She served as Chancellor of the University of York for thirteen years (the first woman ever to do so) and on her retirement was accorded the freedom of that city. She also holds honorary degrees from Oxford, Cambridge, and nine other universities and was awarded the Gold Medal of the Royal Philharmonic Society.

Dame Janet is a member of the Munster Trust, a trustee of the Foundation for Sport and the Arts, as well as patron of the Leeds International Piano Competition and the Elgar Birthplace Trust.

During the late 1970s, Dame Janet Baker worked with Ubaldo Gardini on two major Mozart roles: Vitellia (La clemenza di Tito) *at the Royal Opera House Covent Garden – a production later taken to La Scala Milan – and Idamante* (Idomeneo). *Ubaldo also prepared her for a recording of* Così fan tutte *conducted by Sir Colin Davis.*

'Ubaldo taught me everything I know about the Italian language. It was like a university degree. In those days at Covent Garden – the so-called "golden era" – we had time to do detailed work. Colin Davis and others believed in the need to get the production right and they did everything to attain an international standard. As full-time Italian language coach, it was Ubaldo's job to get our Italian as close to perfection as possible.

'In the practice of singing, language is the great underpinning of the work and the words are as important as the music. As a singer, if you're not secure in handling the language half your power is gone. Now I teach my own students what Ubaldo taught me and I even apply it when I sing in English. It's the legacy of the five or six years I worked with him.

'When the Royal Opera went to Milan in the 1970s with *La clemenza di Tito*, Ubaldo said we'd have to sing the Italian properly, otherwise we would face the derision of the La Scala audience. It was a challenge. But we rose to it and actually impressed them.

'Being an opera singer is like being an athlete. You can't just coast along; you have to put your best into it and strive for excellence. I remember the strict discipline of working with Ubaldo – it was unbelievably hard. He and Colin Davis were a good team. With the conductor at the piano, a scene of about ten minutes would be worked on for perhaps three hours. Ubaldo would deconstruct it and we'd stop at every bar, putting the words and music under a microscope. With all the preparation, all the groundwork, we used to reel out of rehearsals totally stripped of preconceptions.

'Anyone can sing an aria, but few people can bring heart and imagination to the recitative. From Ubaldo I learned all the elements, especially the pacing. Since you don't speak a sentence all the way through to a fixed metre, we learned how to sing in the natural rhythms of Italian speech, first on a monotone, until it was automatic. Then we analysed what we were trying to express.

'After you were confident with the words, Ubaldo left you free to shape the phrase as you wanted and put your own individual stamp on it. Callas was a genius at the recitative. It seemed as if she just spoke it spontaneously – an ability that is the mark of greatness in a singer.

'Ubaldo was a first-rate artist in his own right, uncompromising in his demand that our Italian was accurate. The way he taught the language stayed with me. He expected us to work as hard as possible, and pressured us to do our best. Despite his fanaticism about the language and his immense knowledge, nonetheless, he was very kind and sympathetic to singers. It was the combination of his personality allied to his encyclopaedic mind that got the best from us.'

HILDEGARD BEHRENS
SOPRANO

…as Elettra, *Idomeneo*, Metropolitan Opera House New York

Renowned for her legendary interpretations of the dramatic soprano roles in Wagner and Strauss, **Hildegard Behrens** has performed and recorded throughout the world with the greatest conductors and directors. Born in Varel, Germany, she graduated from the Law School of the University of Freiburg and subsequently studied voice at the city's conservatory. She then joined the Deutsche Oper am Rhein in Düsseldorf, where she came to the attention of Herbert von Karajan. It was her Salome, under the *maestro*'s direction at Salzburg in 1977 that launched her brilliant career.

Miss Behrens' versatility is demonstrated by her forays outside the German and standard operatic repertoire. Most notable are her Tosca (opposite Domingo in a Franco Zeffirelli production for the Metropolitan Opera House New York, and opposite Pavarotti at the Opéra de Paris); her Katerina Ismailova (*Lady Macbeth of Mtsensk* at the Bayerische Staatsoper Munich); along with the world premiere of *Cronaca del luogo*, composed specially for her by Luciano Berio. She is also an accomplished recitalist with a repertoire ranging from Bach and Mozart to Wolf and Elgar.

The discography of Hildegard Behrens includes audio and video recordings of Wagner's *Der Ring des Nibelungen* (Levine and Sawallisch), Berg's *Wozzeck* (Abbado), *Tristan and Isolde* (Bernstein), *Salome* (Von Karajan) and *Der Freischütz* (Kubelík).

Miss Behrens' many prizes include three Grammies along with prestigious operatic awards both in her native Germany and elsewhere. She has received many national honours, most notably the Bundesverdienstkreuz, conferred in recognition of her contribution to German culture.

Ubaldo Gardini prepared Hildegard Behrens for the role of Elettra in Idomeneo *at the Metropolitan Opera House New York – a production that was videotaped, broadcast and recently released on DVD.*

'The first time I saw Ubaldo was in 1982 on television, during a stop-over in Edinburgh on my way to the United States. It was a programme about *Don Giovanni*, with Colin Davis and Ruggiero

Raimondi. They were working on the recitatives, and the way he taught the piece, Ubaldo came across as a very passionate, theatrical musician. I was truly electrified by that programme and have never forgotten it. Then, some time later, I was very happy to see him at the Met when he worked with us on *Idomeneo*. Once again, he made the recitative seem like a matter of life or death.

'Ubaldo is a rare and unique character, so fastidious about the text that he could sometimes drive the accompanist nearly crazy. I know that his passion can be exasperating – and even put people off – but it didn't bother me. That's because I am a passionate musician myself and not afraid to scream or be freaky or dramatic in the music if it's necessary. Ubaldo was uncompromisingly honest and direct and so was I, and we met on that wavelength. I felt very comfortable with him, we could discuss things.

'I remember when my Elettra was being videotaped and broadcast. It was a Jean-Pierre Brunel production, conducted by James Levine, and came out beautifully. I can't attribute all of that to Ubaldo, but he was an important part of it. Sitting in the prompt box, he was so involved, almost acting the role himself, that at times he looked ready to jump out!

'We also decided during that period to do some other work together. By then, I had already performed at La Scala and been invited to Bayreuth, so I was well established. Yet because of his knowledge, along with his very personal vision and concept of things, I incorporated many of his suggestions and technical ideas into my performance. In these he was very forthright – even temperamental – but I didn't mind. He was really driven as a musician – not from vanity or extravagance, but for the musical and theatrical impetus. If he was wrong on some points or his interpretation at odds with someone else's, so what? Nobody's perfect. As a coach, he was absolutely in control – yet too much a musician not to listen to an alternative opinion.

'After my last Elettra, I moved on with my heavy repertoire of Wagner, and so Strauss and Mozart became a rarity for me. But I will never forget Ubaldo and our rehearsals together. His enthusiasm for the human voice was electrifying and infectious. He inspired me. As you can see, despite my short encounter with him – not even a couple of years – he made quite an impact on me.'

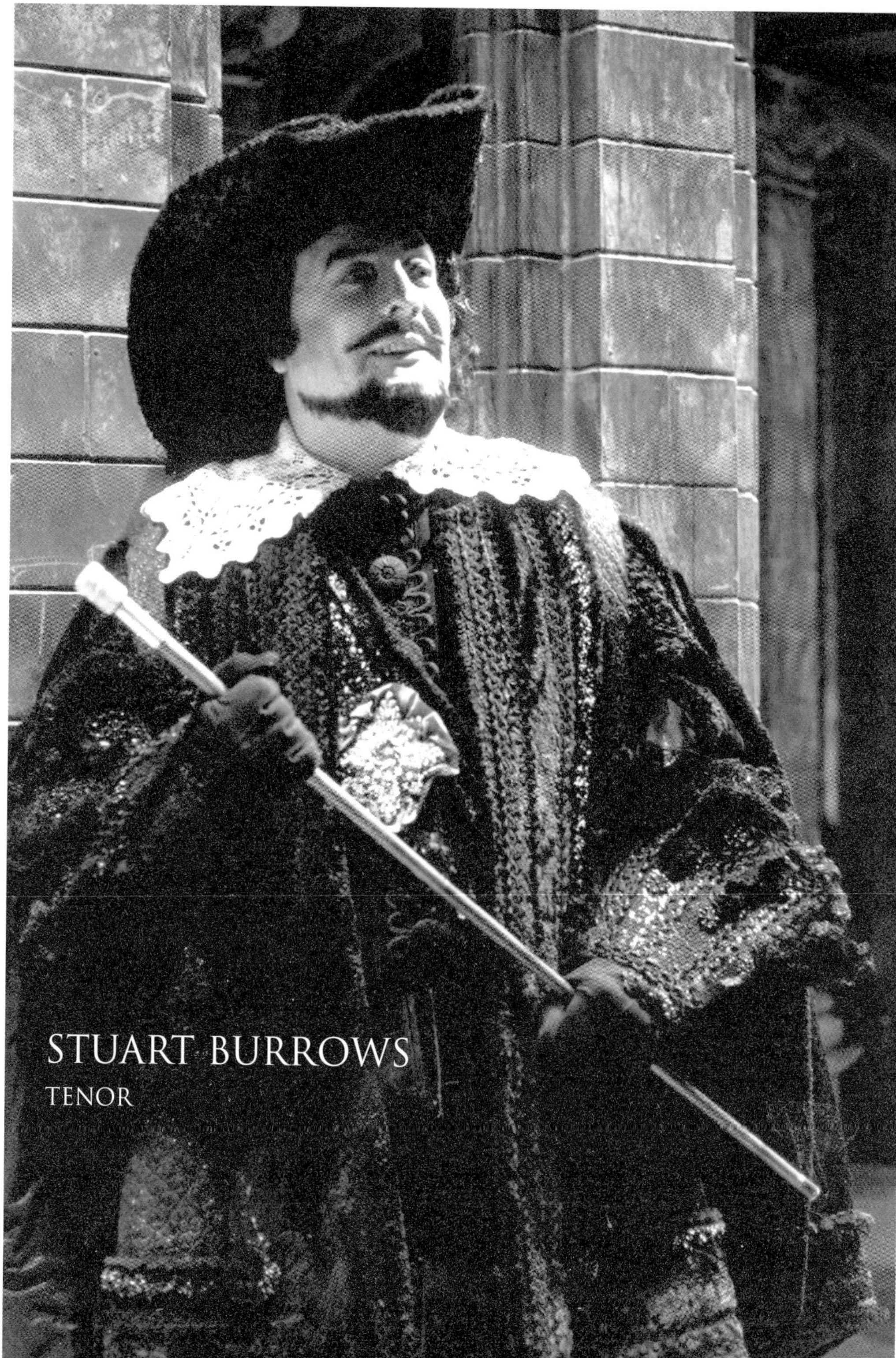

...as Don Ottavio, *Don Giovanni*, The Royal Opera House Covent Garden

An internationally-renowned tenor, **Stuart Burrows** was born in Pontypridd, Wales. He made his stage debut with the Welsh National Opera in 1963 as Ismaele in *Nabucco*. His first international engagement was in 1965 at the Athens Festival in Stravinsky's *Oedipus Rex*, at the request of the composer himself. In 1967 he made his first appearance at the Royal Opera House Covent Garden. During his long career he has performed at the world's leading opera houses and sung most of the major tenor roles, including Don Ottavio, Ernesto, Rodolfo, Beppe, Tamino and Pinkerton.

No stranger to the concert platform, Stuart Burrows has filled New York's Carnegie Hall on several occasions, giving performances under Solti, Barenboim, Mehta, Ozawa, Bernstein and Ormandy.

In addition to his own BBC TV series, *Stuart Burrows Sings*, he has appeared in several opera films, most notably *Faust*, *La Bohème* and *Rigoletto*.

Mr Burrows has made many acclaimed recordings including *Die Zauberflöte* and *Eugene Onegin* (Solti) and Berlioz' *Requiem* (Bernstein). He has received honorary doctorates from the University of Wales and his *alma mater* Trinity College, Carmarthen, where the Stuart Burrows' International Voice Award was established in 2006. He is also in demand to give masterclasses and as an adjudicator at international singing competitions.

Among the roles Stuart Burrows worked on with Ubaldo Gardini at the Royal Opera House Covent Garden are: Ottavio (Don Giovanni), *Tito* (La clemenza di Tito) *and the title role in* Idomeneo. *Numerous recordings prepared with Ubaldo include two versions of* Don Giovanni *and* La clemenza di Tito.

'When I first worked with Ubaldo as a visiting artist at Covent Garden, I was already established in my career, flying from place to place, passing over the Atlantic sometimes eight, nine, ten times a year. My debut at the Royal Opera House was in the John Copley production of *Don Giovanni* with Colin Davis and Geraint Evans.

'As a language coach, although he was obviously well-read, Ubaldo never overstepped his remit. Nor did he involve himself in the production side, unless he was asked. He would be there at the rehearsals, and when he heard somebody incorrectly pronounce an Italian phrase he would mark it on his score and deal with it later. Fortunately, the Welsh thing comes into it. Ours, too, is a singing language: double consonants and pure vowels, we have the lot. If you sing Welsh well, you can cope with Italian.

'At that time Ubaldo was part of the new team at the Royal Opera House. It was refreshing. Superficially, the House was no different, I suppose, from any other – except that there was a very healthy attitude to rehearsal. But with experienced singers, you did it once or twice and that was it. For example, an ensemble rehearsal would consist of Colin conducting and Ubaldo monitoring our singing. One of them would point things out and we would all observe the corrections and employ them next time round.

'With Colin Davis, Ubaldo and the singer, it was a "tri-partite" situation. We all relied on each other because the ultimate aim was perfection. Ubaldo developed a good rapport with everyone he coached and treated every singer as unique, regardless of their level of experience. In my career I've probably worked with over forty sopranos, all with beautiful voices, but all different. You could see the machinations of his mind, endeavouring to get the best out of each.

'The wonderful thing was, if you learnt an opera with someone like Ubaldo, you knew you could go anywhere and sing it, not once, but many times. It had, if you like, the stamp of a master. It's mainly thanks to him that I've had compliments about my Italian in different opera houses. The combination of Ubaldo's total involvement and industriousness plus his sense of humour made coaching sessions extremely pleasurable. He was a joy to work with and as long as he was smiling and happy so was I.'

...(kneeling) in the title role, *Don Carlos* (with Piero Cappuccilli as the Marquis de Posa), Salzburg Festival

Occupying a privileged position in the music world, **José Carreras** grew up and studied in Barcelona where he also made his debut in 1970 at the Gran Teatre del Liceu in *Nabucco* and *Lucrezia Borgia*. His meteoric rise to fame resulted in early engagements at the world's most prestigious opera houses and festivals, including La Scala Milan, the Metropolitan Opera House New York, the Vienna State Opera, the Royal Opera House Covent Garden and Salzburg and Verona.

His repertoire includes over sixty operas, most notably: *La Bohème, Tosca, Don Carlos, Carmen, La forza del destino, L'elisir d'amore* and *Un ballo in maschera*. He has also sung with renowned orchestras under conductors such as Maazel, Bernstein and Sinopoli, and performed leading roles in operatic films for television and cinema.

With a diverse concert repertoire of over 600 song titles, ranging from baroque to contemporary music, José Carreras has given recitals in the world's most famous concert halls, including New York's Carnegie Hall. His vast catalogue of recordings has led to numerous national and international awards.

In 1992 Mr Carreras was engaged as Musical Director of the Olympic Games held in Barcelona. ('The Three Tenors' concerts with his colleagues Plácido Domingo and Luciano Pavarotti are now legendary.) Since 1988, he has presided over the José Carreras International Leukaemia Foundation.

José Carreras worked with Ubaldo Gardini on numerous roles at the Royal Opera House Covent Garden, including Alfredo (La Tra viata), *Nemorino*, (L'elisir d'amore), *Manrico* (Il Trovatore) *and Rodolfo* (Luisa Miller). *Maestro Gardini also prepared him for recordings of these operas, along with* La Bohème, Un ballo in maschera, I Lombardi alla prima crociata *and others.*

'The 1974–75 opera season, the year that my international career was launched, was very important for me. I was making my debut at the Met, La Scala, Vienna – and at the Royal Opera House Covent Garden where I first encountered Ubaldo. This was in our rehearsals for *La Traviata,* after which I was performing at least one production a year there. Most of the time Ubaldo was involved.

'I was still very young then, in my mid-twenties, so I needed someone with his experience to help with my roles. He was always precise, meticulous and rigorous. I had to ensure that I gave each word its due importance. He was also very concerned about making the right pause in the recitative, so that the meaning of every phrase was clear.

'Ubaldo was a very good right-hand man for Colin Davis, both for stage performances and for recordings. He knew the repertoire and all the traditions – which he'd learned from great artists. He wasn't the usual kind of coach who just makes notes and corrects your pronunciation. He was an important part of every production because he had so much to contribute. For him, the libretto was crucial because opera is drama.

'Ubaldo never imposed his own interpretation of a role on the singers. He made suggestions and you felt that he saw himself at the service of the librettist, the composer, the conductor. He had the intuition to know what every artist is capable of, both their strengths and their limitations. He insisted that when performing a role, we singers must use our individual talents and personalities.

'For recordings, he was at every rehearsal and treated every session as though it were a first night at La Scala. I remember him putting all these coloured pencils on the table and constantly noting new ideas that could improve our performance. His interest and his effort made him indispensable.

'Ubaldo was also fun to work with and we had a fantastic time together. I hold him in great affection. We need people like him in the world of opera: people who know the traditions, who are passionate about music, and for whom their job is a real vocation. Unfortunately, we don't have enough of them now.'

ELIZABETH CONNELL
SOPRANO

...as Isolde, *Tristan and Isolde* (with Susan Parry as Brangaene), English National Opera

One of the world's leading dramatic sopranos, **Elizabeth Connell** made her debut at the Wexford Festival in 1972. The following year, to celebrate the opening of the Sydney Opera House, her performance in *War and Peace* led to an ongoing, special relationship with Opera Australia. Meanwhile, after five years as a member of the English National Opera in London, she went on to establish a successful, international freelance career.

Miss Connell has appeared at many of the world's great opera houses including Covent Garden, Paris, Vienna, Berlin, Munich, New York and Milan in a wide repertoire ranging from *Lohengrin, Tannhäuser, Der fliegende Holländer, Tristan und Isolde, Der Ring des Nibelungen, Elektra* and *Ariadne auf Naxos,* to *Nabucco, Macbeth, Attila, Don Carlos, Fidelio, Jenůfa* and *Peter Grimes*. She has had successful collaborations – both operatic and in concert – with conductors such as Abbado, Muti, Sinopoli, Giulini, Sawallisch, Mackerras, Downes, Davis, Maazel, Levine, Ozawa and Elder. She has sung at major festivals including Bayreuth, Salzburg, Verona and Glyndebourne.

Her many recordings include Donizetti's *Poliuto*, Verdi's *I due Foscari*, Wagner's *Lohengrin*, Schoenberg's *Gurrelieder*, and *lieder* by Schubert.

Elizabeth Connell studied the following roles with Ubaldo Gardini: Viclinda (I Lombardi alla prima crociata) *and Leonora* (Il Trovatore), *both at the Royal Opera House Covent Garden.*

'Ubaldo was the first Italian coach I ever had – this was at the London Opera Centre in 1970. Before that, instead of "Dove sono", I would sing "*Dovay sonouh*" with all the English diphthongs because I didn't know any better. I arrived from South Africa thinking I knew everything, but soon realised how wrong I was. We performed operatic extracts at various times during the term – in total three operas a year. Later, I worked with him at the Royal Opera House Covent Garden, where my debut was in *I Lombardi.*

'Ubaldo was passionate about his language. He spoke the line and then got you to repeat it, so that the sounds and rhythm became fixed in your ear. You did it so many times that it was something like muscle memory, a way of singing that never leaves you. One of his other concerns was the preparation. When you were speaking the line, even before you'd uttered the first word, he would stop you and say, "You weren't ready. I could tell just by looking at you." Sometimes he couldn't explain exactly how to correct the problem, so you did it half a dozen different ways until you got it right.

'Singers are often reluctant to spend time on such details. They want to hear their beautiful voices immediately. Ubaldo helped you understand that to get the pronunciation and inflection of the language right you first have to speak the line several times – an exercise that separates the professionals from the amateurs. You then must do what I call away-from-the-piano work. Take the phrase, "Ben io t'invenni o fatal scritto," from the beginning of Act II of *Nabucco*, where Abigaille discovers that she's not Nabucco's daughter. Translated literally it means, "I'm very happy I have found you, oh fateful document". There's nothing in the score to help you know how to perform it. He expected you to do your own research into the character by reading the libretto carefully.

'Singing the phrase one has to take into account both the emotion of the subtext and an interior monologue along the lines of: "I'm glad I found you, fatal bit of paper. Now I know what's going on and who I am. I've found my birth certificate and it doesn't say I'm Nabucco's daughter, after all." To get those two bars correct with every element intact takes a lot of time and solitary preparation.

'Technically, you have to make the "*n*" of "*Ben io*" a single "*n*" but that of "*invenni*" a double – sung "*Inven ni*" and carried on the breath. The "*ben io*" is elided in such a way that it is not doubled and the "*io*" not begun with a glottal stop. To sing words with double consonants like "*invenni*" and "*scritto*" perfectly, Ubaldo taught me to think of the violin with its down- and up- bows. The long bows are the vowels and the change from one to the other represents the consonants.

'In my own teaching I use Ubaldo's analogy with the violin. He used to say, "Just remember my name, *Uuuuubaaaaaaldooooo*

Gaaaardiiiiiiniiii. Don't finish with a short '*ni*', continue the sound to the end of the [imaginary] bowing as, *Uuuuuubaaaaaldoooo Gaaaardiiiiiniiiii*".

'The main contribution Ubaldo made to my subsequent career was confidence. One of the plusses that came out of my work with him was when I did *Così fan tutte* at La Scala with Riccardo Muti – who's also passionate about his own language. Whereas he was very critical of the men's Italian, when we (Ann Murray and I) started to sing, he turned to the *répétiteurs* and said, "These girls know what they're doing". Because we had been taught by Ubaldo, our Italian was *perfetto*.'

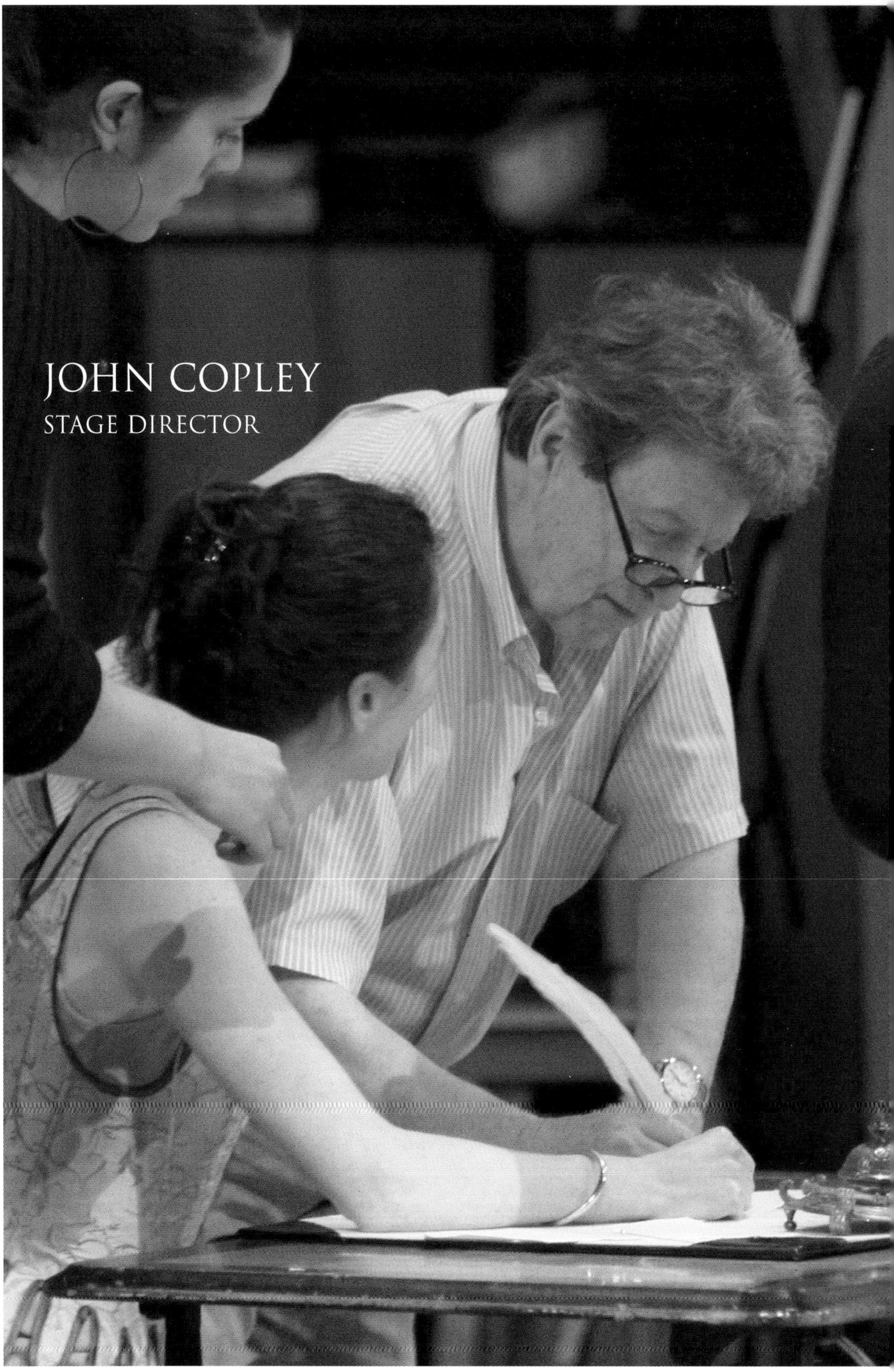

...at work on a scene from *Le Nozze di Figaro*, student production at the Royal Academy of Music, London, 2007

John Copley is one of the world's busiest opera producers. When he was Resident Director at the Royal Opera House Covent Garden he worked on many new productions with such notable conductors as Sir Georg Solti, Sir Colin Davis, Carlos Kleiber and Sir John Pritchard. Among his greatest successes were his stagings of Mozart's *Le Nozze di Figaro* and *Così fan tutte*, works that remained in the repertoire for over twenty years. His acclaimed 1970s production of *La Bohème* is still performed. He has also directed for the English National Opera, working with renowned artists such as Sir Charles Mackerras and Dame Janet Baker.

Mr Copley's overseas engagements include productions with major American opera companies, including the Metropolitan Opera House New York, Chicago Lyric Opera, San Francisco, Santa Fe, Dallas and San Diego. He was for many years a regular producer with the Canadian Opera Company Toronto. He has directed more than twenty-five productions in Sydney and Melbourne.

European engagements include *Macbeth* for Greek National Opera (Athens Festival), *Madama Butterfly* and *Otello*. He returned to Athens in 2001 for a new production of *Il corsaro*. He has also directed in Munich, Berlin, Geneva, Brussels, Amsterdam, Drottningholm, Stockholm and Gothenburg.

John Copley enjoyed the contribution of Ubaldo Gardini to his many productions at the Royal Opera House Covent Garden, including Così fan tutte, Don Giovanni, Il Trovatore, Le Nozze di Figaro *and* Madama Butterfly.

'Although I had been studying Italian I never really felt confident enough to speak it. But, when I started directing at Covent Garden's London Opera Centre in 1960, I needed a better level and had been supplementing my course at Berlitz with private lessons from Ubaldo.

'When we began working together, producing operatic extracts, Ubaldo achieved great things with the *pronuncio*. Jani Strasser (from Glyndebourne) came to see us, and pointedly asked who taught them the Italian, because I couldn't have done it.

'When you're doing a production you've always got people of varying linguistic levels coming in. So, you need to have good language coaches. (Even I'm careless when they're not there because I'm not at all fluent.) But I can tell immediately if a singer doesn't have the right pronunciation. And we English are terrible: we're both sloppy and lazy. We don't think that other languages are important – the Americans are better.

'Ubaldo couldn't bear it if the Italian was wrong. When he came to Covent Garden lots of singers didn't understand what they were singing and it was often gibberish – or worse. I'll never forget a famous occasion in *Madama Butterfly*, when Sharpless tries to guess Butterfly's age, and should have sung "Quindici anni" (fifteen years). But instead, it came out as "quindici ani," (fifteen arseholes)! Sharpless didn't know or didn't bother to pronounce the double consonant [an:ni].

'However, Ubaldo could also be terribly exasperating. We were doing *Figaro* and he was like a terrier. There were a couple of people who were trying exceptionally hard to get it right and not doing very well – but at least they were making the effort. There's no point in aiming for an impossible 120 per cent if it's not there. But Ubaldo often would.

'Along with ensuring we sang our consonants properly and vowels pure, we had to roll our "*r's*". "*Figaretto, Figaretto*," he would scream. He was a perfectionist – though not always clear on how to achieve something. He could also be more explosive than other coaches who might take a singer aside and tell them privately what needs correcting.

'However, I think that if they're honest, other top-ranking coaches would disagree very little with Ubaldo's views on opera. Thirty years on, I still consider him world class. I don't think anybody with that knowledge would ever not be in the top league. Language coaches these days are often pompous, dry or academic – not theatrical, passionate people like Ubaldo.'

ILEANA COTRUBAS

SOPRANO

...as Antonia (with Plácido Domingo as Hoffmann), *Les Contes d'Hoffmann*, The Royal Opera House Covent Garden

Born in Romania, **Ileana Cotrubas** studied at the Bucharest Conservatory and the Vienna Academy of Music, making her debut as Yniold at the Opera Romana in Bucharest. After winning international singing competitions in Hertogenbosch and Munich, she was engaged for three years at the Frankfurt Opera. Other international contracts soon followed, including at the Royal Opera House Covent Garden and the Vienna State Opera – along with festivals in Salzburg, Glyndebourne and Florence.

With a repertoire that encompasses most of the major soprano roles, Miss Cotrubas has performed in the world's leading opera houses and under the most distinguished conductors. At the Metropolitan Opera House New York she has appeared as Mimi, Gilda, Violetta, Micaela and Tatyana, among others. Her acclaimed interpretation of Violetta at the Bayerische Staatsoper Munich under Carlos Kleiber has also been recorded for Deutsche Grammophon.

Her work away from the operatic stage is equally impressive. In concert halls including the Musikverein Vienna and Carnegie Hall New York, she has given *lieder* recitals and performances with great orchestras. Her celebrated recordings include *Le Nozze di Figaro, Die Zauberflöte, L'elisir d'amore, Alzira, La Traviata, Rigoletto, Les Pêcheurs de perles, Carmen, Manon* and *Louise*.

In 1990 Miss Cotrubas retired from performing to devote her time to the education and guidance of young talented singers. The year 1998 saw the publication of her book, *Opernwahrheiten* [*Truths in Opera*], in which she takes a stand against the manipulation of opera productions by stage directors with scant respect for the intentions of the composer.

Ileana Cotrubas worked on the following roles with Ubaldo Gardini: Suzanna (Le Nozze di Figaro, *Glyndebourne*) *along with Violetta* (La Traviata), *Adina* (L'elisir d'amore) *and Mimi* (La Bohème) – *all at the Royal Opera House Covent Garden. He also prepared her for recordings: Despina in* Così fan tutte (*Davis*) *and Violetta in* La Traviata (*Kleiber*).

'I had the chance to work with Ubaldo Gardini at exactly the right moment in my career. It was the 1970s and I was already familiar with the artistic standards at some of the major German opera houses, the Vienna Staatsoper, the Salzburg Festival and at Covent Garden. It had become obvious to me that quality depended not only on the artists, but also on a number of people whom the audience never sees. *Maestro* Gardini – I have never called him Ubaldo – present at every rehearsal in Covent Garden was at that time one of those "spirits behind the scenes".

'He wasn't easy but I liked his approach. He reminded me of Constantin Stroescu, my singing teacher at the Conservatory of Music in Bucharest – a demanding, severe, but exceptionally cultured man, with a refined musical taste. He, too, was never satisfied.

'Sure, Mr Gardini was the Italian language coach but he was also equally knowledgeable about other elements of the opera – the culture of the story and the period, the style, the characters and so on. He was a real musician, what they refer to in France as a *chef de chant*. He was passionate about the repertoire, and a few great conductors understood that and knew they could learn a lot from him. I think he's a genius in his own way, a crazy one maybe, but a genius, nonetheless. What he gave us was of great value.

'It was a wonderful period. I remember with great pleasure the Decca recording of *Così fan tutte*, where he had a lot to say about the role of Despina. However, what I didn't like very much was the way he tried to bring out the salacious meanings in some of the Mozart operas. We know all about that – the relationship between Mozart and Da Ponte, and their enjoyment of *double entendres*. I remember he and Colin Davis – and generally most of the other men in the cast – laughed a lot at these. But I preferred to leave the ambiguities as written in the score, and I just told him so.

'Our work on *La Traviata* dates back more than a quarter of a century, and many of the ideas and suggestions he gave me I now think of as my own. But what I particularly recall were his knowledge and instructions about *portamento*. He would explain how this stylistic feature is an important element of *bel canto* and how its proper use depends on such considerations as the words of the libretto, their sense and place in the musical phrase, and the dramatic content.

(This swooping up to a high note is one of many so-called "operatic traditions" introduced by famous but thoughtless singers, often as an easy solution to technical problems.) The part of Violetta I had previously prepared for new productions in Vienna and Munich, as well as for a revival of the Visconti at Covent Garden. But when I got the offer to record it for Deutsche Grammophon with Carlos Kleiber I knew I needed *Maestro* Gardini again, to bring me nearer the ideal of "my" Violetta. So I asked him to give me private lessons at my home in Sevenoaks, Kent, where I lived at that time.

'As for Ubaldo's personality, I found him very sincere and in his approach to art, totally without ego. He didn't try to impose his ideas on us singers. He communicated what he wanted often in a physical way, such as by acting it out, singing the phrase, or just facial expressions. You could feel his genuine musicianship. To learn from someone like that, artists must be open to his teaching. You had to really understand him and want to go deeply into what the role demanded. I also believe that to make sense of what one's teacher is trying to convey one has to be like a sponge. The conviction of "I have to believe him and must do what he is saying" is also part of one's talent.

'When we were working on something, he would return again and again to a word, and the next, then the whole phrase, and finally go over it all once more until by persuasion he got what he wanted. Of course, it takes a lot of time and nerves, but either you are as committed as him or you're not. You also need the preparation, the knowledge, the discipline and respect for the profession, and to be as cultured in the music. That's why I say that not many singers could cope with his kind of driven perfectionism.

'I've been lucky in my career to have collaborated with some fantastic teachers – and Gardini belongs up there in the ranks of the greats. Today's young singers could do with the help of coaches like that for pronunciation, for style, for phrasing – for everything. It's a pity that he's not working in Europe so much these days. There aren't many coaches who have that all-round musicianship.'

RYLAND DAVIES

TENOR

...as Enéas (with Diana Montague as Parséis), *Esclarmonde*, The Royal Opera House Covent Garden

In a career spanning over forty years, **Ryland Davies** has firmly established himself as one of Britain's most versatile and best-loved tenors. From the start, his beautiful lyric voice has made him a mainstay of the world's major opera venues, most notably the Royal Opera House Covent Garden, the Metropolitan Opera House New York, Deutsche Oper Berlin, Houston Grand Opera, and Netherlands Opera.

His major roles, with distinguished conductors, include Arbace (*Idomeneo*), Monostatos (*Die Zauberflöte*), Le Duc (*Chérubin*), Aumonier (*Les Dialogues des Carmélites*), Don Basilio (*Le Nozze di Figaro*), Alcindoro (*La Bohème*), Monsieur Triquet (*Eugene Onegin*) and Reverend Horace Adams (*Peter Grimes*).

More recent performances include Guillot (*Manon Lescaut*) for Los Angeles Opera, Alcindoro (*La Bohème*) at the Royal Opera House Covent Garden, and Hauk-Sendorf in the new production of *The Makropulos Case* for the Paris Opéra-Bastille.

The roles on which Ryland Davies worked with Ubaldo Gardini include Ferrando (Così fan tutte, *Glyndebourne*), *Don Ottavio* (Don Giovanni), *Fenton* (Falstaff), *along with the title roles of* Don Pasquale *and* Il barbiere di Siviglia *– all at the Royal Opera House Covent Garden. Ubaldo Gardini also prepared him for a recording of* Idomeneo *with Sir Colin Davis.*

'Ubaldo Gardini played an enormous part in my career. I first met him in 1967 while working on Glyndebourne Touring Opera's production of *L'elisir d'amore*. He is responsible for both my singing of Italian and my love of the culture.

'It's essential for opera singers to know how to pronounce the Italian language properly. But Ubaldo went beyond that. He showed us how to sing the libretto idiomatically so that the double consonants were used to full dramatic effect – then, how to render the singles correctly and not double them by mistake. A good example is the Countess's recitative in *Le Nozze di Figaro*, "Prima amata" (at first he loved me). Here Ubaldo would encourage the soprano to almost *not* sound the "*m*" in both these words. This was not only to avoid the trap of doubling them, but especially to give extra *legato* to the phrase, suggesting even more the languishing heart of the neglected wife. Then there is the Italian "*s*" of *Così fan tutte* which is a very crisp sound. To pronounce the "*s*" simply as a kind of "*z*" is wrong. In fact, it is more a combination of both – "*Coszì*".

'Ubaldo also taught us how to relate the language to the musical line, when to be percussive, as in fast patter sections written *staccato*, and how (like string players) to "bow" the voice through *legato* passages – without "stopping" it.

'While he was quite proud of my progress Ubaldo was never afraid to be frank – helped by his unique Italianate imagery. I remember during the recording of *Idomeneo*, he said to me about some of my recitatives, "Ryland, you know, it is very good what you do." But then he added, "I must tell you, be careful. Sometimes you're singing with absolute *nobilità*, but other times it has become rather like the style of a street singer." The reason was too much *portamento*. He believed that sliding about in a grand Mozart opera made it sound weak and in bad taste. "Fai una *portamento* tardi e presto", he would say, meaning, make the *portamento* late and quickly. "Lega la voce", that is, bind the voice, attach the upper note to the consecutive lower one, and so on throughout the phrase, irrespective of the leaps. "Lega, lega si, come la pasta fatto a mano." In other words, just like the pasta made by the hands of an Italian Mamma, there are no holes and no air escaping – now I'm speaking with an Italian accent because I used to imitate him so much!

'When Jani Strasser would remind him we had only six weeks' rehearsal, not six months, Ubaldo had another expression, "Noi dobbiamo lavorare, fino a la fine, come la piede delle mosche." (We must work to the end of the end, to the foot of the fly.)

'Looking back on that period, I'm very grateful that we probably had the best of Ubaldo, when he was young and energetic. It's hard sometimes to put into words all the work he did and what he achieved – the great singers coming out the other side.'

COACHING IN OPERA

COACHING IN OPERA

This chapter is based mainly on interviews with the following: ***John Beeson****, Head of Music, New York City Opera; Assistant Conductor, Metropolitan Opera House New York;* ***Nico Castel****, Staff Diction Coach, Metropolitan Opera House New York;* ***Maria Cleva****, London-based freelance Italian coach;* ***David Gowland****, Artistic Director, Jette Parker Young Artists' Programme, Royal Opera House Covent Garden;* ***Anthony Legge****, Head of Opera, Royal Academy of Music, London and former Head of Music, English National Opera;* ***Antonio Pappano****, Music Director, Royal Opera House Covent Garden.*

Introduction

Tucked away in most opera programmes among the production credits and under the all-embracing title 'music staff' is a list of extremely talented behind-the-scenes musicians. They are the opera company's music coaches – and just as all successful sports stars have experts guiding their protégés to ever-higher levels of performance, opera singers, too, receive special nurturing to achieve their best. Indeed, one-to-one coaching constitutes such an integral part of the several weeks' rehearsal period in international opera houses that 'without it,' says Maria Cleva, 'the show cannot succeed, no matter how brilliant a conductor you have'.

The Versatility of Opera Coaches

Known also as '*répétiteurs*' or 'assistant conductors,' opera coaches, however, need a range of skills probably broader than their sports counterparts. With interchangeable nomenclature and frequently overlapping functions – depending on the needs of the conductor, production and the opera house – their tasks are diverse. These include teaching the principals and chorus their roles, accompanying and taking rehearsals, assisting the conductor in various ways, liaising between everyone, playing keyboard instruments in performance – and sometimes even conducting the orchestra. Finally, since the flawless production that everyone is working towards is not usually in English, a specialised member of the team, the foreign language coach and usually a native speaker, is also on hand to attend to linguistic needs.

Antonio Pappano's summary of a season as part of Daniel Barenboim's coaching staff at the Bayreuth Festival some years ago aptly illustrates the range of responsibilities of the coach/*répétiteur*/assistant conductor. 'You were teaching singers their roles, people who were doing big pieces for the first time, like John Tomlinson doing his first Wotan, or Siegfried Jerusalem also tackling a debut role. You were in charge of making the huge daily schedules for playing the *Ring*. Because all the operas were rehearsed at once, you might be conducting piano rehearsals in one place while Barenboim was working on another opera elsewhere. When he was with the orchestra you often had to help him and be his ears in the auditorium, so that you could offer feedback. At other times he would throw you in front of the orchestra to conduct.'

Indeed, opera coaching is such a demanding profession that many former practitioners, like Pappano himself, have gone on to illustrious conducting careers. These include Herbert von Karajan, Reginald Goodall, Ricardo Muti, Sir Georg Solti, Claudio Abbado and Wolfgang Sawallisch. 'I think in all the cases, our coaching heritage has never left us and it's brought coaching fame, if you like,' Pappano concludes.

It is also significant that several of these great conductors were also accomplished pianists, since the piano is indispensable during the rehearsal process. A 'temporary' accompaniment for singers so they can identify instrumental cues and textures, it has to function as a miniature orchestra – from mimicking specific instruments to creating impressionistic elements, such as laughter or 'flirty' chords. To achieve this the coach/*répétiteur*/assistant conductor needs extra musical and pianistic skills – virtuoso playing is not enough. So along with an intimate knowledge of the score, the music staff may need to create their own versions of the piano reduction so that it replicates the full ensemble as much as possible.

The reason, according to John Beeson, is that rehearsal scores, no matter how detailed, often lack the elements the singer hears in the orchestra. 'If there is a horn cue, even though it's missing from the piano reduction, it must be inserted,' he explains. A typical example might be a page that faithfully reproduces a string section's sequence of fast notes, whereas in reality, what is more audible is a trumpet solo. 'New York conductors expect the *répétiteurs* to adjust the piano reductions accordingly,' he says.

However, coaches also help the singers on a more basic level. Anthony Legge explains the difficulties the novice may face in the transition from piano rehearsals in the studio to orchestral run-throughs on the stage. 'The piano is a very clear and rhythmic instrument. So soloists may find when they first sing with the orchestra, they can't hear it properly and their singing drags, or they miss their cues. We help them to understand why the conductor may be shouting at them and try to sort out any problems.'

Why is Coaching just for Opera Singers?

This is to do with both the voice and the nature of opera itself. Because their musical instrument is located inside the body, singers do not actually hear the sound as the outside world does. (They may not even realise they can be out of tune.) The coach, therefore, acts as an 'auditor', analysing such elements as the quality of the tone (too hard or not beautiful enough) – or the language (incorrectly pronounced or lacking emotional connection to the text). Added to that is a kind of conundrum whereby even when singers think they are singing loudly the audience may still not be able to hear them. Antonio Pappano explains: 'The voice should always be focussed towards the back of the hall. But it's not a question of volume. The secret is soft singing that projects.'

Then there is the complexity of the performance itself, which nowadays requires a range of talents to deliver it convincingly. Not only must singers know the music, understand and learn the foreign-language libretto and be able to sing it beautifully, but because opera is essentially music-drama, they – even the chorus – must also be good actors. The static performances of the past, with the main emphasis on the singing, have given way to today's more theatrical productions.

Maria Cleva stresses how all the technical skills needed for opera singing can only be acquired with expert coaching. 'One mustn't forget that as opposed to the straight theatre where actors may be in the same play for several weeks or months – even if rehearsing another simultaneously – opera singers do only ten performances and usually in a foreign language. They may be preparing other roles at the same time, in another language, then almost immediately, they're off to the next production, in a different language again. So they do about twenty different shows a year, meaning they may have twenty different operas in their heads within a twelve-month period – in a range of languages.'

How Opera Coaching has Changed

As with other aspects of opera production, coaching has also undergone changes since Ubaldo Gardini's tenure at the Royal Opera House Covent Garden. Back then, individual daily coaching in both music and language was the norm. Generous resources enabled music staff to respond fully to the soloists' various musical needs.

Many of the 1960s and 1970s generation were not as musically proficient as those of today. In fact, singers were often described as the 'late starters' of the music profession. Even though they may have learnt the piano or another instrument, their natural singing talent and the potential of their voices were often not discovered until their late teens – or beyond. Some even lacked formal musical education that necessitated note-by-note teaching.

Whatever their musical background, singers of that era enjoyed the luxury of extended support in preparing their roles. Kiri Te Kanawa's year-long coaching at the Royal Opera House for her debut as the Countess Almaviva in *Le Nozze di Figaro* is one example. According to Antonio Pappano, other distinguished beneficiaries of lengthy coaching include John Tomlinson, Anne Evans and Gwynne Howell – all protégés of the noted British conductor, Reginald Goodall. Rita Hunter's three-years' rehearsing with him for Brünnhilde in *Die Walküre*, exceptional though it was, exemplifies, nonetheless, that 'golden age'. The outcome was a generation of singers completely 'at home' – both physically and musically – in their characters, able to give confident and masterful portrayals and reprise them anywhere. Anthony Legge explains, 'If you keep performing the role, you get to know it thoroughly. But nowadays you get merely one chance.' It is all connected with the internationalisation of opera, the variety of ways of encountering it, and the transformation of the infrastructure.

While opera venues and the repertoire have expanded, the turnover of productions has accelerated, and audiences have increased, the number of permanent companies, however, has declined. Thus, the demands on performers have never been greater. Usually contracted on a short-term, production-by-production basis, they are expected to be both word- and note-perfect when they arrive at the opera house to start rehearsals. As a result, instead of seemingly limitless preparation time, in-house coaching is reduced and some of the music team, including the language coach, are hired just for individual shows.

However, on the plus side, to cope with this new situation, changes have occurred in the vocal departments of music conservatoires. Most now have opera departments offering professionally-geared courses which usually include language skills and stage experience. Then after graduation, the exceptionally talented can receive further practical training in the full-time Young Artists' programmes provided by many opera houses.

Today's rising stars enjoy other advantages. As a result of globalisation, talented singers, irrespective of their country of origin, have access to both overseas studies and prestigious international competitions. In addition, the growing popularity of opera around the world, the increasingly imaginative ways of presenting it, the mushrooming of small independent companies, summer seasons and festivals, all guarantee that graduates nowadays start their careers better equipped than their predecessors and with more performing opportunities.

Ironically, though, despite all this lively, international opera scene – the modern phenomenon of aspiring singers criss-crossing the globe in search of courses, competitions and jobs – the role of the language coach is more vital than ever. While there may be no problems with musicianship and vocal technique, they still need linguistic help. According to John Beeson, 'now we have an influx of singers, such as from Russia or Asia, for whom the culture of the opera is not native, coming over to Western opera houses and trying to sing from a text in an unfamiliar foreign language.'

Kiri Te Kanawa in the 1971 production of *Le Nozze di Figaro*, Royal Opera House Covent Garden. Her successful debut as Countess Almaviva was due in no small measure to extensive preparation by the music staff.

The Libretto – Genesis of the Opera

David Gowland, as Artistic Director of the Royal Opera House Young Artists' Programme, with the luxury of more time than in the professional company, never lets his singers forget how in the creation of the opera, the music is the composer's response to a pre-existing libretto. So first, he recommends that they translate it into their own individual languages. This, he explains, 'ensures not only the necessary emotional involvement in the role but also equips the singers with the energy and confidence to give a performance that is convincing and engaging'. The next step in the rehearsal process is a detailed read-through of the drama to clarify the plot and the relationships between the characters.

Coaches will also provide background information on the culture of the opera. In Gowland's case, his preparation for a production of *La Traviata*, for instance, would involve reading the original Dumas play along with research into the history of the period. Ubaldo Gardini cites two examples of the cultural insights he offers in Japan. For *Cavalleria rusticana* it is the meaning and significance of the *pasquale* (Easter). In the case of *Le Nozze di Figaro*, he teaches how the opera is not a simple love story but rather has a political underlay wherein the plot represents a profound challenge to the social order – one of the reasons the French play on which it is based was initially banned. He also has to explain the shocking (by today's standards) European feudal custom whereby the lords of the estate (in this case, Count Almaviva) could exercise their feudal rights to bed a servant girl (Susanna) on the eve of her wedding.

Performance Style in Opera

Another function of coaching is familiarity with opera's history and performing traditions. Depending on their historical period and genre, all operas have their own distinctive styles, the details of which are not always evident in the libretti or scores.

So what are the stylistic details with which coaches need to be familiar? They include such technicalities as the manner of singing the aria, the position of the voice, the way to enunciate certain vowels, and even how long to hold a *fermata* (pause).

Maria Cleva provides a simple example of how one stylistic feature, the *portamento* [a chromatic slide or glide over a series of notes], is treated differently from one opera to the next. Comparing Mozart and Puccini, she cites Susanna's aria, 'Deh vieni non tardar', (*Le Nozze di Figaro*) and Mimi's, 'Sì, mi chiamano Mimì', (*La Bohème*). She explains how in Mozart the *portamento* has to be done with finesse, more like a 'super *legato*', so that the audience cannot hear all the chromatics. In Puccini, by contrast, it is used for emotional effect, with the slide more obvious and dramatic.

However, it can be difficult for coaches nowadays to acquire such background knowledge. In the past, according to John Beeson, music staff having coached for famous conductors would have inherited an artistic tradition, which they would then pass on to the singers in their charge. He cites the example of conductors at the Met and elsewhere until the 1970s – such as Luigi Ricci, Roberto Massialo, Tullio Serafin, Giancarlo Gavazzeni, Karl Boehm and Walter Townsend – who had worked variously with Verdi, Puccini, Richard Strauss and others. (Beeson himself has such a fortunate link. At the start of his career he played the piano in the studio of Carolina Segrera who had sung at Milan in the 1920s, worked with Toscanini, and taught at La Scala's school of singing. He also played for Maria Callas.)

Other coaches, too, exemplify the importance of artistic lineage. As a singer himself, Nico Castel claims he can tutor a style even for roles he has never sung. 'For example, I can teach a tenor Cavaradossi, or how to phrase the aria, "Recondita armonia", and others. I've learnt them through being on the *Tosca* stage, doing another part.' As the daughter of the great Fausto Cleva, conductor at the Metropolitan Opera House New York and a 'protégé' of Toscanini, Maria Cleva spent much of her childhood in the 1940s and 1950s listening to her father conduct the greatest works in the repertoire. Ubaldo Gardini had a similar, musically formative background in his native Italy. Opera has always been part of his life, never more so than when he was at the Teatro Comunale in Florence, and other Italian opera houses, learning on the job.

A scene from New York City Opera's *Don Pasquale* with Kevin Glavin (centre) as the Don – the culmination of meticulous preparation by the music staff

Without a direct link to the past, however, today's coaches have to acquire their stylistic knowledge by a more academic approach. In addition to musicological and literary sources, vintage recordings are invaluable, states John Beeson. He provides the example of the Callas discography, which he regards as an important operatic legacy. Aside from her own instinctive genius for making the music come alive in a particular way, they are what he describes as 'a veritable goldmine of what people like Serafin and Gavazzeni taught her'.

Singing in a Foreign Language

According to Antonio Pappano, while being able to sing in foreign languages is one of opera's most basic requirements that singers should wholeheartedly embrace, it is also particularly challenging. On the other hand, he sees all languages as predominantly sensual entities, each with its individual allure and musical possibilities. By way of example, he lists powerful foreign words that he considers more evocative than their English equivalents: the lift in the Italian word '*bella*', (beautiful); the length and a languor in the French '*la fleur*', (flower); and the poignancy implicit in the German word '*Wahn*', (disillusionment).

Pappano concedes that the ability to sing competently in different languages depends not only on the singers' capabilities but also on their linguistic backgrounds. Southern Europeans will be most comfortable with other Latin-based languages and able to sing Italian with 'panache'. But they would probably need help with Russian and Czech, he says. A northern European, on the other hand, confident in English and German may not be so at ease with Italian and French, adding reassuringly that 'Anglo-Saxons who speak only English in everyday life need not despair. They are remarkably adept at singing in a range of foreign languages'.

The Italian Language – Theatrical but Difficult

Most people involved in opera production agree that Italian, with its pure vowels, wide range of colour and potential for expressiveness, is one of the most beautiful languages to sing. 'Italian opera, when every word is brought to life, can be very exciting,' continues *Maestro* Pappano. 'The job,' he explains, 'is to exploit the dramatic possibilities of the language.' This particularly applies to the recitative which has to carry the plot.

He cites the opera *Don Giovanni* with its 'acres of recitative' in which lines must be delivered with clarity and conviction, and paced according to the ebb and flow of the action and the characters' emotional states. Knowing when to be aggressive, passive, hushed or loud, and 'how to string these together to motivate the next aria or the next entrance for the orchestra' cannot be achieved without the input of the language coach.

However, not all artists are aware they may need help. Because so much of the operatic repertoire is in Italian and they enjoy singing it, many singers have a false notion of their proficiency, according to Nico Castel. In reality, he explains, it is the language that gives English speakers the most problems.

The myriad of complex pronunciation rules are just the start. Whereas those in German are very precise, Italian, by comparison, can be vague, even contradictory. Antonio Pappano concurs about the difficulties, commenting that conductors like himself, Muti, Abbado and Gatti spend a lot of time on one-to-one Italian coaching.

Understanding the libretto with its linguistic intricacies adds to the problems. Even Nico Castel, when translating his some 150 libretti, found those in Italian the most exacting of all – even more so than the *Ring*, he acknowledges. He explains how librettists at the time of Verdi, such as Piave and Cammarano, loved to convolute phrases. His simplest example occurs in Germont's opening line in *La Traviata*. 'D'Alfredo il padre in me vedete' is literally translated as 'Of Alfredo the father in me you see', which simply means, 'I am Alfredo's father'. Castel claims that the line would be more straightforward in French or German.

He continues that the texts in Rossini, or Mozart's lesser-known operas, contain even more complicated language than those of Da Ponte. 'Sometimes,' he says, 'it can take a while to find the main verb, which is in there somewhere. However, things get easier in the *verismo* operas – late Puccini, Mascagni, Leoncavallo – where the dialogue is more conversational and, hence, easier to understand.'

Spicy *double entendres* – especially in Mozart operas – can also create a particular challenge, and a coach needs to be fluent in the Italian language, literature and culture in order to ensure that the singers understand and convey them. 'They are definitely in the subtext,' says Maria Cleva, 'whether a director uses them all or not.' She gives some examples of the (more printable) sexual witticisms. In Act I of *Così fan tutte*, Despina's query about the officers, 'Son giovani, son belli, e sopra tutto hanno una buona borsa... ?' (Are they young, handsome, and above all have they got a good purse?) is a reference to both a money and 'personal' purse [or codpiece]. In the same opera, Guglielmo's Act I aria: 'E come ognun vede, sia merto, sia caso, abbiamo bel piede, bell'occhio, bel naso' (and as one can see, whether by chance or merit, we have a good foot, good eyes, good nose) also has a sexual connotation. As does Count Almaviva's declaration in Act I of *Le Nozze di Figaro*, 'Ah no, Susanna, io ti vo' far felice.' (Ah, Susanna, I want to make you happy.)

The Role of the Language Coach

Just as opera singers are rarely polyglots, neither is it necessary for the language coach to be multilingual. Although Nico Castel is an exception in that he speaks six languages fluently, the expertise of most coaches is usually confined to a thorough knowledge of one or two. Additionally, they must also understand vocal physiology. 'You must know the sounds of the language in your own mouth and body, in order to reproduce them for the singer,' according to Mr Castel.

The system he follows at the Metropolitan Opera is typical of that of most international houses. After the first rehearsals to assess the performers' handling of the language, he can quickly identify various linguistic needs. For artists who are quick on the uptake, on-the-spot corrections will suffice, he says. Then there are others who will require full coaching sessions. In the final category are a minority who place a low priority on the language and only seek help at the last moment. Singers like these, he concludes, so set in their ways, are beyond redemption. 'So you just throw up your hands and say good-bye.'

As a former lyric tenor at the Met, Castel, who has sung more than 200 roles, explains that being a singer, and going beyond the confines of basic language coaching, he can readily identify vocal problems. Referring to the difficulties singers may have when straining after a high note on a particularly awkward vowel and singing flat, he might suggest changing the vowel a little to get more space. In the worst cases, where 'they're singing in the cracks between the notes or turning green on their high pitches', he may recommend a return to the voice teacher. 'These are all things that only one singer can tell another.'

The Importance of Good Diction

The language coach is also responsible for ensuring that the words are articulated clearly, projected out over the orchestra and audible throughout the opera house. There are occasions when opera-goers may see the performers emoting powerfully enough, but because of poor diction they have no idea why.

Might the advent of surtitles be to blame? Mr Castel vehemently refutes this charge and retorts that the titles are installed for the benefit of the audience, not the performers. He insists that language skills will always include good diction, especially in the case of singers with the potential to become top-ranking soloists. They know that eventually they will be recorded and their performances put down for posterity, and that bad or unclear pronunciation would lessen their chances. 'Artists don't want that blemish on their careers,' he asserts. 'So everybody tries to do the best that they can. That is why Ubaldo worked so hard in Covent Garden and Glyndebourne to ensure that the talented singers who were coming along at the time – and who made those great recordings – got the language right.'

© Marty Sohl

Coaching is not restricted to soloists – a full-cast scene from *Orfeo*, Metropolitan Opera House New York

The Psychological Aspects of Coaching

To deliver a realistic performance before a live and (usually critical) audience opera singers need an extraordinary range of skills: exceptional talent, total confidence, strong physical stamina, steely nerves and complete command of the singing, language, emotion and stagecraft. Coaches sensitive to their artists' psychology can help them not only achieve their best but also remain at the peak of their form in this ultra-competitive profession. They offer support, belief, motivation – and an ability to massage egos. According to John Beeson, 'opera singers are a distinctive group. Forty percent of the coach's job is knowing how to deal with all the different kinds of personalities.'

Despite their high artistic achievements and, in many cases their superstar status, opera singers are, nonetheless, only human and can suffer from a range of problems that may adversely affect their performance. David Gowland says that coaches need to know why singers feel nervous or have lapses of confidence, and how to manage them and put them at their ease. 'There are some singers who after all the rehearsal process will remember only the flaws, the bad notes. Coaching them away from the conductor for an hour can work wonders in restoring self-belief.'

Anthony Legge affirms that a good relationship between coach and singers is vital in the quest for optimum performance. This ranges from giving advice and reassurance to offering positive feedback, helping the artists achieve their potential, and at the same time steering them clear of unsuitable repertoire.

Of course, there is always the risk that singers will become excessively reliant on their coaches. When Gardini left the Royal Opera House for New York in 1981, some of his 'protégés' acknowledge that they felt let down. He had helped them to achieve so much that they doubted their ability to survive artistically without him.

Despite such a close working relationship, no good coach encourages over-dependence – rather, after a certain point the artist must become self-sufficient. Opera coaches, for all their various talents and skills, are not expected to be Svengalis.

BIOGRAPHIES

John Beeson

Born in Atlanta, Georgia, **John Beeson** studied music theory and composition at Yale University. He has been assistant conductor at the New York City Opera since 1977 and Chief of Music Staff and Principal Coach since 1990. He has held various posts as assistant conductor, including for the Opera Company of Boston, the Lyric Opera of Chicago, the Spoleto Festival, Artpark Opera (where he prepared Wagner's *Ring* Cycle for Christopher Keene) and San Francisco Opera. John Beeson has been a master coach for The Adler Fellows at San Francisco Opera, as well as a regular guest coach for the Vocal Ensembles of the Canadian Opera Company in Toronto and the New York City Opera National Company. In recital he has collaborated with such artists as Renata Scotto, Teresa Kubiak, Robert Merrill and William Walker. His career has included some years as a faculty member at the Juillard Opera Center, New York.

Nico Castel

Born in Portugal to multi-lingual parents, **Nico Castel** emigrated to the USA in 1948, where he studied singing and established a successful international career as an opera singer, becoming a specialist in over 200 tenor roles and an accomplished linguist in six languages. He has for years been considered an authority on multi-lingual lyric diction both in the USA and internationally, and is currently in his 38th season at the Met, on the roster both as an artist and as Staff Diction Coach. His expertise has taken him to worldwide opera companies, major universities and conservatories. In addition to his post at the Metropolitan Opera, he is also a staff member of the Santa Fe Opera, the Juilliard School of Music, the Mannes College of Music, the NUOVA opera project in Edmonton, Canada, and the Spoleto Arts Symposia in Spoleto, Italy. For fourteen years he was associated with the International Vocal Arts institutes in Israel, Mexico and China. Nico Castell is known internationally for his volumes of 150 libretti of major operas and operettas. He is also the author of two recently published books for singers, *The Nico Castel Book of Ladino Song* and *A Singer's Guide to Spanish Lyric Diction.*

Maria Cleva

Daughter of the distinguished conductor Fausto Cleva, **Maria Cleva** began her singing career in Italy at the Teatro Coccia of Novara as Suzel in *L'amico Fritz* in 1961. She studied at the Giuseppe Verdi Conservatory in Milan and at the Manhattan School of Music, New York. She later worked in the USA and Europe, with appearances at the Massimo Palermo and Teatro San Carlo Naples, the Teatro São Carlo Lisbon and, in Germany at opera houses including those of Munich, Stuttgart, Mannheim, Dortmund and Cologne. In 1983 she joined the Royal Opera House Covent Garden as Italian Language coach. She has also worked for many other British companies including Opera North, Glyndebourne and Welsh National Opera. She has assisted Sir Colin Davis as language coach at the Vienna State Opera, Munich National Theatre and the Semperoper in Dresden. She has also worked for many recording companies and now teaches at London's Royal College of Music, Royal Academy of Music and National Opera Studio, as well as at the Mariinsky Academy in St Petersburg.

David Gowland

David Gowland studied at the Royal College of Music in London, winning the Ruby Hope and Major van Someren Godfrey prizes for piano accompaniment, and at the National Opera Studio, where he is now a visiting tutor. He joined the Glyndebourne music staff in 1987 and continues there as a senior coach. As former Head of the Music Staff at the Grand Théâtre de Genève from 1989–96, he assisted conductors such as Tate, Patané, Thielemann and Elder. He has worked regularly with many international opera companies and festivals as assistant conductor/senior coach, including productions with the Opéra National de Paris, Netherlands Opera, Rome Opera and the Aix-en-Provence, Salzburg and Wexford festivals. He was senior coach on Wagner's *Ring* cycle under Jeffery Tate in Australia. Concert work has included appearances at the Edinburgh and Aldeburgh Festivals, for the BBC Proms and on television and radio. Mr Gowland has been associated with the Young Artists' Programme at the Royal Opera House since its inception in 2000 and also regularly accompanies its singers in recitals of both song and opera. He has also accompanied leading soloists such as Barbara Bonney, Amanda Roocroft and Cecilia Gasdia.

Anthony Legge

After studying music at Oxford University and further studies at London's Guildhall School of Music and Drama, **Anthony Legge** went on to the London Opera Centre where, at the end of his course, he was invited to join the permanent staff. He has worked with all the major British opera companies including the Glyndebourne Festival, and many abroad. He is in demand as a coach to many international opera singers and has played in recital with the UK's leading artists, including Dame Janet Baker, Dame Anne Evans, Sir Thomas Allen and Robert Tear. His recordings include two CDs accompanying Linda Finnie in recital and an appearance as harpsichordist on the award-winning Deutsche Grammophon recording of *The Rake's Progress*, conducted by Sir John Eliot Gardiner. He has been assistant conductor on many other opera recordings and frequently appears for the BBC in this capacity for opera broadcasts. For some fifteen years he was Head of Music at English National Opera and is now their Music Adviser. He is regularly in demand as a judge for major singing awards and as the author of *The Art of Auditioning* has given many masterclasses on the subject. He is also the author, with Mary King, of *The Singer's Handbook, a Guide for Aspiring Singers*.

© Sheila Rock

Antonio Pappano

Born in London, **Antonio Pappano** moved to the USA at the age of 13. His work as *répétiteur* and assistant conductor led to worldwide engagements. In 1987 he made his debut at the Norwegian National Opera Oslo (*La Bohéme*), where he was appointed Musical Director in 1990. He was Music Director of Théâtre de la Monnaie Brussels from 1992 to 2002. His conducting debut in Vienna in 1993 was followed by others at the Metropolitan Opera House New York (1997) and Bayreuth (1999). Antonio Pappano's many recordings include *La Bohème*, *La Rondine* (Gramophone Record of the Year 1997), *Trittico, Tosca, Don Carlos, Tristan und Isolde, Wintermärchen* and *The Turn of the Screw*. He became Music Director of the Royal Opera House Covent Garden in 2002, the following year gaining the Olivier Award for Outstanding Achievement in Opera. In addition to his work at Covent Garden, he is also Music Director of the Accademia Nazionale di Santa Cecilia, Rome.

MEET THE ARTISTS

Biographies & Interviews Part Two

MARK ELDER
CONDUCTOR

...with the BBC Singers, Symphony Chorus and Orchestra at the Last Night of the Proms, Royal Albert Hall, London, 2006

Mark Elder is Music Director of the Hallé Orchestra and also works regularly with other world-renowned ensembles. In the UK he enjoys a close association with both the London Philharmonic and the Orchestra of the Age of Enlightenment. He was Music Director of English National Opera from 1979 to 1993, and has been Principal Guest Conductor of the BBC Symphony and City of Birmingham Symphony orchestras. For many years Mark Elder has appeared annually at the BBC Prom concerts in London including, in 1987 and 2006, the internationally-televised Last Night. Since 2003 he has appeared at the Proms with the Hallé Orchestra.

He conducts regularly in prominent international opera houses, including the Royal Opera House Covent Garden, the Metropolitan Opera House New York, the Paris Opéra, the Lyric Opera of Chicago and Glyndebourne. He was the first British conductor to conduct a new production at the Bayreuth Festival. Other international conducting engagements include the Berlin Philharmonic, Munich Philharmonic, Chicago Symphony and Boston Symphony orchestras.

Mark Elder has made many recordings with major British ensembles including the Hallé, London Philharmonic and City of Birmingham Symphony orchestras, as well as guest engagements with the London Symphony Orchestra and others.

He was awarded a CBE in 1989. In 2006 he was named Conductor of the Year by the Royal Philharmonic Society.

Mark Elder was répétiteur for rehearsals with Ubaldo Gardini at Glyndebourne, the Royal Opera House Covent Garden and the Wexford Festival. He later worked with him as a conductor on Rigoletto *and* La Bohème *(Royal Opera House) along with* Il Trovatore *and* Aïda *at the English National Opera.*

'My career as a conductor had not started when I first met Ubaldo. In 1968, while still at Cambridge, I had a holiday job as a "walk-on" at Glyndebourne. I was the second sheriff in *Anna Bolena* and he was there coaching singers. I was immediately fascinated by opera's combination of music and drama, and from then on, I avidly studied operatic scores from the dramatic perspective.

'When I joined the staff of the Royal Opera House as *répétiteur* in 1970, I often played for Ubaldo's coaching sessions. He very soon opened my eyes, ears and heart to the relationship between music and the word, and on a wider plane, the connection between music and the pulse of human existence. At that tender age, I sensed that I needed someone who could push me forward in my musical development. Ubaldo and I became close friends and colleagues, and a few years later when I conducted at Covent Garden for the first time, he was there to help me.

'Although he was employed as the main Italian coach, it became clear to me that he was much, much more – a true musician, a genuine artist. I realised I could learn a lot from him – if I could only keep up with him, and be as demanding of myself as he was of us all. He taught me about the style of the music of his country – what makes it tick and how in performance, precision and rigour are as vital as passion and flair.

'Certain fundamentals were emphasised, for example, how singers and conductors alike have a responsibility for the musical integrity of a production. He showed me that Italian composers need good interpreters, and how fragile and vulnerable these great works are in less-than-good performances. Conductors can be the worst perpetrators! They must hold the ebb and flow of the music in their hands, and show commitment and intensity.

'Ubaldo had devised a way of helping non-Italians understand the power and beauty of his own language, and how they should articulate it. There are many other people who can teach the same thing, and do it very well, but his passion and energy were infectious.

'Those of us who studied with Ubaldo realised he was sharing something that, if we could only grasp it, would enhance our music-making. He'd spend twenty minutes on one word – but when it was right, we heard it and understood why. He certainly helped me to improve my own aural awareness. But he also gave us the courage to take risks and thereby extend ourselves. This was encapsulated in the word "slancio" – for which there is no adequate English translation. The nearest probably is, "Come what may, I am going to bring off this phrase with verve and panache."

'I learned more about conducting from him than from anyone else. First and foremost was the challenge of the control of the music's pulse and how the conductor must maintain the musical tension throughout the entire opera. You can slacken or quicken the pulse, but always organically, not jerkily. In addition, Ubaldo explained so much about what lies hidden in these great works, their connection to their past, their originality. He showed me how they were monumental.

'Throughout the 1970s I was very aware that Ubaldo felt constrained by the fact that his official position as language coach did not allow him a full outlet for his creative energy. He dreamed of being able to conduct operas himself, and even to be responsible for directing the productions. Being thwarted in these ambitions – endlessly trying to persuade hesitant Anglo-Saxons to perform in his mother tongue – probably made him feel that his wings were clipped.

'So many years and performances later, many of us miss him, his stamina and dedication, dearly – and daily! I can still recall exactly the things he said, and I still treasure the quest for the highest standards that he started in me.'

…as the Marschallin, *Der Rosenkavalier*, The Royal Opera House Covent Garden

American soprano **Renée Fleming** continues to thrill audiences with a voice described as the 'gold standard of soprano sound', a meticulous and dazzling gift for characterisation, and a rare stylistic versatility. Awarded the *Chévalier de la Légion d'Honneur* by the French government, her superb artistry has also inspired the 'Renée Fleming Iris', along with master chef Daniel Boulud's dessert, 'La Diva Renée'.

Miss Fleming has performed in concert and opera on the world's most famous stages, including the Paris Opéra, the Mariinsky Theatre St Petersburg, the Sydney Opera House, La Scala Milan, the Vienna State Opera, the Royal Opera House Covent Garden, the Kennedy Center, Carnegie Hall, and at her 'home' venue, the Metropolitan Opera House New York. A two-time Grammy winner, Miss Fleming has also earned seven Grammy nominations plus a Classical Brits Awards in 2004 and selection as Female Artist of the Year for her Outstanding Contribution to Music. Her recent recordings include *Homage – The Age of the Diva*, the Grammy-nominated-CD of Strauss' *Daphne*, *Sacred Songs*, *Renée Fleming: Handel*, the jazz recording *Haunted Heart*, and the movie soundtrack to *The Lord of the Rings: The Return of the King*.

In addition to her work with Ubaldo Gardini on La Bohème *and* Le Nozze di Figaro *which feature in her interview below, Renée Fleming also worked with him on several recitatives and arias while a student at the Juilliard School of Music, New York.*

'During my first year at Juilliard I was fortunate to meet Ubaldo Gardini. My time there was fundamental to my artistic development, and Ubaldo's guidance was important, in part because his commitment was palpable and he made each of us believe that we could succeed. He had a particularly colourful way of expressing himself both in language and with gesticulation, which helped us realise our potential to create drama in music and on stage.

'I remember specifically Ubaldo's work towards a natural approach to singing. He was fond of saying "if it looks funny, it's wrong" – a phrase which I continue to use today, since the mirror often provides the first indication of physical tension and/or unnecessary muscular involvement when singing. He also spent a good deal of time helping me with "Dove sono", the Countess's aria from Mozart's *Le Nozze di Figaro*, which was to become extremely important in my early career. In pursuit again of a more natural appearance and sound, he helped me find a way to keep the high notes within the line of the phrase and to resist the natural compulsion to push at the top, by saying repeatedly, "Why do you want to bang that note?".

'I was grateful also to have his coaching for the role of Musetta in Puccini's *La Bohème*, which I sang in my first semester at Juilliard. Too many teachers accept the limitations of their students, but Ubaldo saw my potential and was willing to push me past the extreme inhibition I felt as a shy young adult in my early twenties, so that I could play her character. At one point he shouted in frustration "walk across the room and swing your hips", as I was surely the most demure Musetta who had ever set foot on a stage! I felt at the time that Ubaldo Gardini was investing a huge amount of his energy, hope and talent in me. It gave me confidence and a sense of validation that I was indeed on the right track – which I have tried to realise to the fullest. We never forget our early mentors, and although our time together was short, Ubaldo had a tremendous influence on me, for which I'm still grateful.'

GWYNNE HOWELL

BASS

...as Duke Bluebeard, leaning against his castle's seventh door in *Bluebeard's Castle*, English National Opera

The Welsh bass **Gwynne Howell** studied at the Royal Northern College of Music, Manchester. A member of the Royal Opera House Covent Garden since 1972, he has sung most of the major bass roles with the company. He has also enjoyed a long association with the English National Opera where his many roles have included Hans Sachs, Gurnemanz, King Philip II and Duke Bluebeard. His international career has included performances in New York, Chicago, San Francisco, Santa Fe, Paris, Geneva, Hamburg, Munich and Cologne. In concert he has worked throughout the world with conductors such as Abbado, Giulini, Muti, Bernstein, Boulez, Barenboim, Levine, Haitink, Mehta, Davis and Ozawa. His many recordings include Mahler's Symphony No 8 with Ozawa, *Messiah* with Solti, *Tristan und Isolde* with Goodall, and Beethoven's Symphony No 9 with Masur.

Recent engagements include Schigolch (*Lulu*) and Dansker (*Billy Budd*) for English National Opera; productions of *Pelléas et Mélisande, Manon Lescaut, Don Giovanni, Le Nozze di Figaro* and *Otello* for Glyndebourne; along with the Old Convict in *Lady Macbeth of Mtsensk*, and the world premiere of *The Tempest* by Thomas Adès, for the Royal Opera House, which he reprised in Santa Fe in 2006.

Gwynne Howell was awarded the CBE in 1998.

The roles Gwynne Howell worked on with Ubaldo Gardini include Il Re and *Amonasro* (Aïda), *Monterone* (Rigoletto) *and Timur* (Turandot), *all at the Royal Opera House. Ubaldo Gardini also prepared him for a recording of* L'elisir d'amore *with Sir Colin Davis.*

'I came to the Royal Opera House during the 1970–71 season to sing *Salome* with Solti. For someone who'd arrived from virtually nowhere, suddenly, here I was with a contract. Later, when I had to play the King in *Aïda*, it was my first foray into Italian repertoire – and my initial encounter with the fanatical (and later I was to realise), the fantastic Ubaldo Gardini.

'Working with Ubaldo was the best academy you could ever have. What he gave were one-to-one master classes, and on reflection, I know that my career would have been impoverished if I hadn't had that opportunity. When you were coached by him, you felt not just imperfect but that you had to be an unusual species to survive the barrage of demands that he would inflict on you.

'I had no particular aspirations. Anyhow, back then aspirations were dangerous. The singing world was dominated by the "stars" of the day, Jon Vickers, Gwynneth Jones, Joan Sutherland, Geraint Evans, Peter Glossop. You couldn't ever imagine joining their ranks.

'The Davis era at Covent Garden was certainly a golden age – the result, I think, of long rehearsal periods. (There isn't the time for such lengthy coaching today.) I suppose we were lucky – and so was Ubaldo – because all the people that he taught there did go on to have big careers. That was the time when the Royal Opera House – rather like a premier league football club – had twenty-five top singers on contract, plus a team of other "players" below, all good enough to step in.

'What were the most relevant aspects of technique that Ubaldo taught me? First and foremost, I would say, the importance of clear diction. His way of training English-speaking people to sing in Italian was to over-emphasise the words. I will never forget my first coaching session in *Aïda*. The first phrase we worked on, the King's "Alta cagion v'aduna", will stay with me forever, we did it so many times. Like your National Service [Army] number, it's fixed in your brain. I've never forgotten that phrase because Ubaldo was at the same time teaching me the importance of *bel canto*. So for the first hour and a half we did three words, how to join them together – in speech. I hadn't yet sung a note. Taking that long to learn just three Italian words, I thought at the time, didn't augur well for my future as a singer.

'Even when you got it right, he couldn't leave it. You'd have to do it a few more times, to show it wasn't just luck – and therein lies the variable. You'd get it right, then wrong, then you try to get it right again. Now it's only nearly right, wrong again. You needed patience, humour and infinite energy. You felt like a punchbag.

'I came to realise that speaking a phrase first, then intoning it before singing it, is an excellent technique when learning a role. As a result, more voice comes out. They weren't just Italian lessons, they were singing lessons.

'Aside from his trademark personal score covered in colourful hieroglyphics, he'd also mark ours. I've still got my copy of *Aïda* with his phonetic symbols, joined together to show how they should be sung in the Italian way. Ubaldo was my grounding in *bel canto* and the payoff was a continued contract at the Royal Opera House and my ongoing work with him as my career developed.

'I remember how he taught me to maintain intensity without necessarily being loud. People think you don't need the same support if you're not singing full voice. But you do. Training with him meant that you could do anything with the voice. It was like plasticine, you could shape it as you wanted because it had such a secure core. You just worked with Ubaldo and then someone would comment on the long lines of clear words you'd just sung, seemingly all in one breath – which is, in fact, *bel canto* at its best.'

...as Octavian, *Der Rosenkavalier*, Teatro di San Carlo Naples

Anne Howells made two notable debuts while still in her mid-twenties: as Erisbe in Cavalli's *L'Ormindo* at Glyndebourne, and as Flora in the Visconti/Guilini *La Traviata* at the Royal Opera House Covent Garden. Her career has subsequently taken her to almost every major opera house and concert hall in the world. She was recently awarded Honorary Membership of the Royal Academy of Music, London (Hon RAM).

The directors with whom Miss Howells has worked include Sir Peter Hall, Nicholas Hytner, John Schlesinger, Jean-Pierre Ponelle, Günther Rennert and John Copley. Distinguished conductors include Sir Colin Davis, James Levine, Sir Georg Solti, Silvio Varviso and André Previn.

Miss Howells is especially noted for her portrayals of Dorabella (Metropolitan Opera House New York, Lyric Opera of Chicago, Royal Opera House Covent Garden and Glyndebourne); Mélisande (Scottish Opera, Royal Opera House); and Concepcion (*L'heure Espagnole*, Amsterdam and Opéra-Comique Paris). At the Royal Opera House, she has also sung Giulietta, Zerlina, Despina and Cherubino. Her contemporary repertoire has included *The Rising of the Moon* (Glyndebourne), along with Searle's *Hamlet*, Tippett's *The Knot Garden* and Harrison Birtwistle's *Gawain* (Royal Opera House). She sings the role of Octavian on the Solti/Schlesinger Royal Opera House DVD of Richard Strauss' *Der Rosenkavalier*.

Anne Howells worked with Ubaldo Gardini at the Royal Opera House Covent Garden on the following roles: Cherubino (Le Nozze di Figaro), *Dorabella* (Così fan tutte) and *Annio* (La clemenza di Tito) – *the last of which later toured to La Scala Milan and was filmed for video.*

'When I started working with Ubaldo, I already spoke Italian. What he taught me was how to apply what I knew to music – which is quite different. My first experience of his coaching was in the chorus at Glyndebourne and, after that, at the Royal Opera House in 1970 for my debut in a sizeable role, Cherubino. We spent over an hour and a half on a page of music, because according to Ubaldo, it's not only a question of pronunciation, but also of detail and style.

'Ubaldo was a monster with the recitative, but it paid off. He insisted that it must be light and conversational as if it's the first time you're thinking, hearing and singing it. In preparing an opera, it's the element that needs most work and good conductors have special "recit" calls. The composers put the chords there as sort of guideposts, but it's got to be effortless and have variety.

'I regard Ubaldo as the *doyen* of Italian coaches. Once I'd done something successfully, he'd be complimentary – a huge thing coming from him. He'd come around to the dressing room and say, "It's goin' well. You've remembered what I told you. *Brava, veramente brava*. If you're singin' like that, I'm tellin' you those Italians will be pullin' up their stockins." (He could never pronounce his "g's".)

'It's difficult being a language coach. You're the most unpopular person because everyone is concentrating on their vocal technique, their sound, and how they look in their costumes. But unless you get the language right, you can leave all the rest at home. Sometimes, though, if our coaching was cut short, we were glad because it gave us some peace and quiet. Ubaldo used to drive people nearly insane because he was such a perfectionist. When you were on stage trying hard, a conductor telling you something important, making you repeat the phrase, and with all sorts of worries about your singing, then the last thing you wanted was Ubaldo coming up and correcting your Italian.

'Once I went to sing Despina in Los Angeles and San Francisco, in Peter Hall's fabulous *Così fan tutte*. The first day I was told, "Miss Howells, your Italian call will be at 2:30 this afternoon." I said, "Excuse me, I don't do Italian calls. First of all, I'm too old, and I know the role extremely well. More importantly, I've studied it with Ubaldo Gardini. Need I say more?" Which was not the right attitude, I suppose. But after I'd learned it with Ubaldo – I wouldn't work on the language with anybody else.'

EUGENE KOHN

ACCOMPANIST & CONDUCTOR

...during the Gardini years in New York with sopranos Licia Albanese and Aprile Millo, Metropolitan Opera House

As former accompanist to such great artists as Renata Tebaldi, Franco Corelli, Maria Callas and Luciano Pavarotti, US-born **Eugene Kohn** had an impressive start to his career. His conducting debut at the Metropolitan Opera House New York in 1980 was followed by appearances at many of the world's leading venues, including the Vienna State Opera House, the Berliner Staatsoper, the Deutsche Oper Berlin, the Opéra National de Paris La Bastille, the Teatro Colòn de Buenos Aires, and the Teatro del Opera di Roma.

From 1992 to 1997 Kohn was Principal Guest Conductor at the Bonn Opera (his performances included *Der Rosenkavalier*, *Don Giovanni*, *La fanciulla del West*, *Otello* and *Fidelio*), and from 1994 to 2001 he was Music Director of the Puerto Rico Symphony Orchestra. He has also been a frequent guest at Washington National Opera and continues an international guest-conducting career both in opera and symphonic music.

Maestro Kohn can be heard with Maria Callas as her accompanist on EMI's live recording, *The Masterclasses*. He made his professional screen debut re-creating this role in Zeffirelli's *Callas Forever*. He can also be seen as conductor on the following DVDs: *Duetto from the Rome Coliseum*, *Finding Eléazar* with Neil Shicoff, and also *Alagna in Concert*. He has made many recordings with Plácido Domingo – the latest of which, *Italia, ti amo*, received a Grammy nomination.

Eugene Kohn worked intensively with Ubaldo Gardini on Madama Butterfly, Un ballo in maschera *and* La Bohème *at the Metropolitan Opera House New York.*

'I was hired by the Metropolitan Opera as cover conductor in 1979 and made my unscheduled debut in January 1980 conducting *La Gioconda* (with Renata Scotto). This resulted in re-engagements for subsequent seasons. In 1981, *Maestro* Ubaldo Gardini was there coaching the Italian repertoire. Since he liked my talent, and as the Met wanted their young conductor to develop, he was asked to prepare the singers for several of my productions. We also began spending considerable time together away from the opera house. He would use my studio at the Ansonia Hotel for coaching singers, and I would observe with great interest his technique and seemingly unlimited reserve of descriptions and analogies.

'For example, to convey musical energy in a phrase he would walk towards the crook of the piano and stretch his hands apart to suggest an imaginary force field, something like the voltage tension between two electrodes. The singers would translate this intensity into superior breath support, while the conductor would sustain it in space with an equally deep, central body connection.

'Ubaldo taught me as much as anyone about communication in music and about a constant uninterrupted feed of tone components, fluid enough to bridge the gap of even a bow change or the taking of a breath. The goal was a time-stopping and energised extension of intonation, maximizing harmonics and "spin" [resonance] above the fundamental sound. This is something that Maria Callas (with whom I had previously had the honour of working for three years as her accompanist) had tried to impart to me – though her message of reducing vocal tone to pure human emotion was made clearer through Ubaldo's intense metaphors. Both Ubaldo and Miss Callas would consistently forbid the uttering of any sound without vibrato. Their concept of human tonal expression and intensity in all music would prove most useful to me in later years, whether conducting works by Bruckner or Bellini.

'Ubaldo's focus on tonality and its connection to a deeply rooted energy source could infuse the duration of an entire musical period with a single purpose. It led me towards a path of simple listening while conducting, bypassing the intellectual and excluding my sense of judgment. Concentrating like this on the power and beauty of timbre allows the musical composition to unfold and acquire its own expression.

'The opulence and revealing truth present in the tone of the greatest human voices (Tebaldi, Warren, Domingo, Siepi) can transcend our everyday thought processes and speak directly to the spirit. Ubaldo also strove for these qualities in orchestral sound. This may be a common factor in the work of some of history's greatest conductors (such as Toscanini and Furtwängler), who through their uncanny ability to make the orchestra "sing", expressed their love for humanity and for music.

'Ubaldo Gardini is a deeply talented man, transmitting his devotion to the composer, from the heart of the music-maker to that of the listener.'

…as Figaro (*Le Nozze di Figaro*) Tokyo Opera Company

Born in Tottori Prefecture, Japan, **Kazuhiro Kotetsu** is founder and director of the Tokyo Opera Company, an independent organisation. He completed his postgraduate degree at Tokyo Geidai University of the Arts in 1991, followed by studies at the Tokyo Nikikai Opera Studio. A Japanese Ministry of Culture artist's scholarship in 1993 enabled him to travel to Italy, where he won a major prize at the international Valsesia Musica Competition. He was subsequently granted the prestigious Japanese Rotary award to continue his Italian musical education.

Mr Kotetsu's repertoire, mainly for the Tokyo Nikikai Opera Company, includes Dr Bartolo (*Le Nozze di Figaro*), Leporello and Masetto (*Don Giovanni*), Sarastro (*Die Zauberflöte*), Uberto (*La serva padrona*), Giovanni (*Il corsaro*), along with roles in *Tosca*, *Madama Butterfly*, *Fidelio* and the Japanese operas, *Shunkinsho* and *Yuzuru*. In 2005 he performed the role of the Imperial Commissioner in *Madama Butterfly* in Taormina, Italy.

The roles Kazuhiro Kotetsu studied with Ubaldo Gardini include Dr Bartolo (Le Nozze di Figaro) *and Leporello* (Don Giovanni) *at Tokyo Geidai and Tokyo Nikikai.*

'I was 22 years old and had already graduated from Tokyo Geidai when I first met Professor Gardini. In those days the university placed more emphasis on German music – so I was particularly attracted to *lieder* and the operas of Wagner. Until then, like a lot of Japanese, I had always regarded Italian music as easier and lighter. Indeed, if I hadn't met *Maestro* Gardini, I might have had a successful career performing popular Italian arias – and made my life a lot easier [laughing].

'I was fortunate that my teachers at Geidai were exceptionally good. Nonetheless, despite master classes with visiting singers like Carlo Bergonzi and Maria Carbone, I felt I needed to study on a more regular basis. So I started working with *Maestro* Gardini. He wasn't at all dictatorial and encouraged me to approach the music creatively as an artist. His conviction, integrity and intensity made a great impact on me.

'The first piece I studied with him was King Philip's aria from *Don Carlos*. I had lessons a few times a month, each one lasting six hours! Afterwards, we'd have dinner together and he'd keep talking about Verdi. I was a typical Japanese, unable to interrupt and say, "I ought to be going home now", so almost every time, I would miss the last train and have to take a taxi.

'Often in these six-hour sessions, we would get no further than the first phrase. As soon as I would take a breath, *Maestro* would say "No", and for half the lesson I would repeat one passage just to get the breathing right. To be frank, at first I thought the man was mad! However, soon I became aware of the knowledge, passion and sincerity in his emphatic "No". *Maestro* does not give up until his singers get it right – or they give up. (I have to admit there are some in Japan who can't cope and are driven away.) He always says that if a musician can master one page, then he or she can easily complete the whole piece.

'Seeing him consult the various editions of the scores and comment knowledgeably on the differences – and often inaccuracies – exemplified the ideal way to prepare one's role. He also gave me the confidence to find my own voice and to think and question what I'm doing.

'*Maestro* Gardini's perfectionism often involves trying out different ideas until he's satisfied. This is quite unusual in the Japanese operatic world and can be rather disconcerting. Thus, some performers have interpreted his changes of mind during rehearsals as not being true to some perceived tradition. But since he bases his teaching and directing on a solid foundation of knowledge, the *maestro* is entitled to break the rules occasionally – something artists have always done.'

ROBERT LLOYD
BASS

...in the title role, *Boris Godunov*, The Royal Opera House Covent Garden

Robert Lloyd was born in Essex and educated at Oxford University. In 1972 he was appointed Principal Bass at the Royal Opera House Covent Garden, where he has since sung many leading roles. His most recent appearances were in *La fanciulla del West, Simon Boccanegra, Don Giovanni, Die Zauberflöte, Turandot* and *Pelléas et Mélisande*. He has also performed in other major international opera houses, including La Scala Milan, Deutsche Oper Berlin, the Paris Opéra, Netherlands Opera and Chicago Lyric Opera. Productions in which he has appeared at the Metropolitan Opera House New York include *Rigoletto, Parsifal, Die Zauberflöte, Aïda* and *Faust*.

Robert Lloyd has given concert performances with the Cleveland Orchestra (Dohnanyi), the Philadelphia Orchestra (Jansons), the London Philharmonic Orchestra (Haitink), and most recently, the London Symphony Orchestra (Davis).

Featured in several highly successful television productions, Mr Lloyd has also written and presented a number of radio programmes on opera and the voice for the BBC. He has a discography of over seventy audio and video recordings.

Robert Lloyd was created a CBE in 1991.

In addition to preparing Robert Lloyd for his first Don Giovanni, Ubaldo Gardini also worked with him on roles including Seneca (L'incoronazione di Poppea) *and Nettuno* (Il ritorno d'Ulisse in patria) *both at Glyndebourne; Fiesco* (Simon Boccanegra) *at the Metropolitan Opera House New York, and Ramphis* (Aïda) *for the Royal Opera House Covent Garden – all later filmed for video. Ubaldo also coached him for major recordings.*

'Covent Garden seemed to me at first to be a kind of temple. I hadn't had any real training when I went there to sing Masetto in a new production of *Don Giovanni* in 1973, so my first coaching with Ubaldo was a nightmare. He wanted to get this very bright Italian sound with the consonants right to the front. We sat very close, face to face, nose to nose doing one of Masetto's lines. "*No-nna mi-toc carrrrr*", he shouted. "*Nonmitocar*", I mumbled. Wrong. It was "*no-nna mi-toc carrrrr, no-nna mi-toc carrrrr*". We intoned the phrase to each other for the best part of an hour until I got it right.

'Ubaldo was a perfectionist, and was both the best, and possibly the worst, thing that ever happened to me musically. First, the plus side: I was extremely lucky he was at Covent Garden at that time. Without him, it would have been difficult to attain an international standard performing opera in Italian. What he injected was the exact antithesis of that English Oxbridge background – cathedral choirs, and so on – that some of us had inherited. He was like a distillation of what you imagine the Italian character to be: extrovert, loud and totally uninhibited. We, on the other hand, were all very demure, repressed English people. Fundamentally, he was trying to get us to be as Italian as possible. I think his principal battle was to rid us of our reserve. That was easier said than done and made coaching hard work – even for him. He always sweated a lot in these sessions and made copious use of his grey-looking handkerchief to mop his brow.

'Ubaldo believed in *legato* perhaps more than anything else. After working with him I evolved a sort of aphorism that I try to give to students or anybody who will listen. I define *bel canto* as the perfect articulation of the Italian language on a seamless melodic line, in which each word in the sentence is equally important.

'Sometimes Ubaldo took you to the edge of vocal danger. He has shown me techniques I would never have thought of. I remember I sang the first line of the aria in *Simon Boccanegra* which goes, "A te l'estremo addio". The "*A te*" is on the B natural. He asked me to make the note seem as though it came from a different octave. He explained that "at this moment Simon is hurt and proud, and needs a more arrogant sound". I knew instantly what he meant and so I engaged a kind of undertone in the voice. Previously, I'd only been aiming at overtones, as I believed that basses should sing like tenors, for whom high overtones are their stock in trade.

'Along with the Italian language, Ubaldo was a great proponent of what he regarded as the Italian tradition. He didn't seem to bother with dynamic markings or the tempi. While this is anathema to trained English musicians, it can actually be very liberating. Italian singers are often quite disrespectful of what's written on the score – out of time, late on the beat and inventing their own dynamics. But they do have a kind of traditional understanding of the way the music goes. I think Ubaldo brought some of that to his coaching: the feeling that it's the emotion that matters.

'However, the reason I say that Ubaldo was probably the worst thing that happened to me is because some of us felt that the Italian he taught was highly suspect. In the process of trying to eradicate the Englishness from our pronunciation, some of his compensatory Italian sounds were a kind of approximation. For example, he would encourage us to say an Italian "*d*" instead of the usual soft-edged English "t". So instead of "*tutti*", we often ended up saying "*duhdee*". Nearly everybody who was under his influence used false consonants like this. He knew that they were better than what we had been doing before, but native Italians who sang with us couldn't understand the rationale.

'Riccardo Muti used to say to me, "*Sono MuTi, non MuDi.*" At an *Aïda* rehearsal in Munich he stopped me and asked, "Why do you say it like this, Lloyd?" Plácido Domingo was there and said, "It's that guy Ubaldo Gardini at Covent Garden. That's how he tells them to do it. They're all the same". It took a long time to get through that and only by working in Italy did I come out the other side knowing the truth of the matter. After that *Aïda*, Muti never used me again for Italian opera, only for German.

'Looking back, though, I suppose I must concede that Ubaldo did me more good than harm. For people of my generation he is legendary really, and an unsung hero, if you like, though he would probably reject the epithet. I've often thought, though, that I'd like to lay my hands on his score of *Don Giovanni*. It was totally covered with scribbles and annotations of what all the great singers before us had done with the words and the music. It was an obsession with him. I'd love to see it – and now perhaps even add some of my own observations. I've heard a good few *Don Giovannis* in my time.'

© Opera Illinois

...as Zerlina (with Bass Baritone Peter Volpe), *Don Giovanni*, Opera Illinois

The winner of numerous music competitions, **Reveka Evangelia Mavrovitis** began her professional career in such venues as the San Francisco Opera Center, Sarasota Opera, San José Opera and the Santa Barbara Grand Opera. In 1995, she moved to New York where she has performed with the Metropolitan Opera in *Madama Butterfly, La Traviata* and *Suor Angelica*, and distinguished herself in roles including Mercédès (*Carmen*), Rosette (*Manon Lescaut*), Dimitri (*Fedora*) and Olga (*The Merry Widow*). With New York City Opera, she has sung the title role from *Carmen* (subsequently receiving the Lincoln Center Debut Artist Award), Suzuki in *Madama Butterfly*, and the Statue in Lukas Foss's *Grifflekein*.

Miss Mavrovitis made her Carnegie Hall debut in Mozart's *Requiem* and returned to sing the title role in the US premiere of Mikis Theodorakis's *Elektra* in 2000. She has appeared as soloist with numerous orchestras, including the Minneapolis Symphony, San Francisco Pops and the Sacramento Symphony.

As a guest artist at the Festival Lyrique in Belle-Ile, the largest opera festival in western France, Miss Mavrovitis made her European debut in the title role of *Carmen*, returning to sing Cherubino (*Le Nozze di Figaro*) and Flora (*La Traviata*). Other European engagements have included performances at the Opéra de Lyon in France and the Spoleto Festival in Italy.

Reveka Mavrovitis worked with Ubaldo Gardini on various roles in Madama Butterfly *(Tokyo Geidai / San Francisco Opera Center joint production of the Brescia edition). He also coached her for the role of Cherubino* (Le Nozze di Figaro).

'*Butterfly* was such a great experience all around. One of the most memorable moments occurred at the start of our first rehearsal. Ubaldo had his score open, a very old one, and was looking at the first page which was full of different colour markings from all of his past productions. He turned the page once and went back again, over again, back again, all the time shaking his head. I asked him "Ubaldo, what's wrong? What's going on?" "I don't know where to begin," he said. That was something that stayed with me: every time we go to a piece, every time we practise, we must start afresh.

'As someone who is motivated by people wanting detail, I responded to Ubaldo's slow pace of working, it provided time for discovery. When you're creating something, you don't have coaching for an hour and then go to lunch. The true artistic approach is to work until you're satisfied.

'I also learned from him how to teach myself to study. Before I left for Japan I got a call telling me I would be covering Frederica von Stade in San Francisco. It would be my first Cherubino. So I asked Ubaldo, if he had time, would he prepare me. He very kindly made tapes for me. First, he went through the background to *Figaro*. He talked about the history, Petrarch and the structure of Italian lyric poetry that Da Ponte was imitating. Next, he spoke all of it for me, then sat with his pianist and sang through the whole thing. When he did the recitatives, he explained the phrasing and style, telling me to avoid certain things that would be vulgar. I listen to those tapes all the time – even when I'm studying French music.

'One or two people on the Japan tour rather recoiled from Ubaldo's approach. He can contort all he wants, that's just his involvement and emotion; I couldn't care less. You'll hear him on my tapes singing and grunting the orchestral lines. He can't help it, it's inside the connective tissue of his body and has to come out.

'I've been a musician all my life – as a pianist, violist and dancer. I was trained in classical ballet by three very demanding teachers with three completely different styles. So I learned from a very young age, mostly through ballet, that there are many ways to get the most perfect *plié*. Then in the final performance we would all dance together with a kind of uniformity. So it never bothers me when people come with different ways to do things. The important thing is the respect for the artistic creation. There's no doubt, Ubaldo's first love is for the composer and librettist – the people who created the music.'

...as Didon, *Les Troyens*, The Royal Opera House Covent Garden

Born in Sydney, Australia, **Yvonne Minton** moved to Europe in 1961, winning the Kathleen Ferrier prize at the prestigious s'Hertogenbosch Competition (The Netherlands) shortly thereafter. She pursued her studies in London with Henry Cummings and Joan Cross, and in 1964 was engaged by the Royal Opera House Covent Garden, where her roles included Sesto, Dido, Orfeo, Dorabella, Kundry, Brangäne and Fricka. Appearing at all the major European opera houses and at the Bayreuth and Salzburg festivals, Miss Minton was also a regular guest with the Cologne Opera. With the Paris Opéra she took part in the first complete production, subsequently recorded, of *Lulu* conducted by Boulez, singing Countess Geschwitz. She made her American debut at the Lyric Opera of Chicago as Octavian, a role reprised at the Metropolitan Opera House New York.

Miss Minton was also an active concert singer and recitalist performing in leading venues in Hamburg, Paris, Geneva and Vienna, among others. Her many recordings include *Parsifal, Das Rheingold, Die Walküre, Der Rosenkavalier, La clemenza di Tito, La Damnation de Faust, Béatrice et Bénédict, Lulu* and Elgar's *The Dream of Gerontius*. She now gives master classes in the UK and abroad as well as teaching privately.

Awarded Honorary Membership of the Royal Academy of Music London (Hon RAM), Yvonne Minton is also a recipient of the CBE.

Yvonne Minton was coached by Ubaldo Gardini for the following roles at Covent Garden: Dorabella (Così fan tutte), *Cherubino* (Le Nozze di Figaro), *Sesto* (La clemenza di Tito) *and the title role in* Orfeo. *He also prepared her for the following recordings: Cherubino* (Le Nozze di Figaro) *and Sesto* (La clemenza di Tito), *both conducted by Sir Colin Davis.*

'Although my career was mostly in German opera, I always did any significant Italian role with Ubaldo. He coached my entire Mozart, beginning with Cherubino in 1967. I was only 21, green as grass, and hadn't had any Italian training when I came to London. It was very different in Sydney in those days. Although we had great directors, we didn't have a permanent company where beginners could learn their roles. So neither I, nor most of my colleagues who subsequently came over to the UK, were full-time singers. I was a secretary, others worked in banks and places like that, and got time off for their *Messiahs*, opera performances or, occasionally, a tour.

'I hadn't been here long when I met Ubaldo, and until I stepped onto the Covent Garden stage, I hadn't had any proper opera experience. He was just what I needed. When we were rehearsing – and we did a lot – he was always present, making notes so that he could drill us later. We weren't allowed to get away with anything. When we had one-to-one teaching, he came into his own.

'Good coaches inspire you, and working with him was like taking a pill every day. He was a musician – who came to the opera with the cultural background, drama and poetry of Italy. It was like dealing with an Italian Shakespeare.

'We always started with language, and put the music to it later. I preferred that. I wanted to be sure about the text and the enunciation. If you articulate clearly, you don't have to think about such technical aspects as airflow or abdomens. Rather, everything falls into place, you breathe in a calm way and then use the text.

'Words have always fascinated me, how you pronounce them and how they feel. I think if I hadn't been a singer, I would have been an actress. The ensembles and arias in *La clemenza di Tito*, for instance, are fantastic – the way Mozart uses the language with his ravishing music. I'm thinking especially of that very successful Covent Garden production by Antony Besch with Janet Baker and Colin Davis.

'I still have Ubaldo's marks on my *Così* score from when I sang the role of Dorabella. The familiar word "*rubato*" is written with a single "*r*" but we had to give it four! "It's *rrrrrubato*", he would cry. Actually, when you do that, you can feel the whole body saying it with you. Such training is invaluable, and I was never impatient even if it took ages to get my pronunciation correct.

'That era is over now, of course. It's such a pity that today's young singers don't have such intensive language coaching. They just use words and discard them. They don't embrace them like Ubaldo taught our generation.'

EIKO MORISHIMA

ACCOMPANIST & RÉPÉTITEUR

Eiko Morishima is one of Japan's leading opera *répétiteurs* and accompanists for concerts, recordings and broadcasts. Graduating from Tokyo Geidai University of the Arts with a degree in piano performance, Miss Morishima was awarded an artist's scholarship in 1982 by the Japanese Ministry of Culture to study *lieder* with Konlert Richter at the University of Stuttgart.

Miss Morishima is also an accomplished chamber musician, collaborating with many international artists including leading players from the Berlin Philharmonic, Vienna Philharmonic and NHK Philharmonic orchestras. A distinguished harpsichordist, she also plays with the NHK Philharmonic Chamber Ensemble. In 1991, she took part in an impressive eighty performances to mark the 200th anniversary of Mozart's death.

Awarded the Shin Nittetsu Music Special Prize in 1994, Miss Morishima teaches both at Tokyo Geidai and Okinawa University of Arts and Music.

Eiko Morishima worked with Ubaldo Gardini at Tokyo Geidai, the Nikikai and the Nasa opera companies on the following productions: Idomeneo, Le Nozze di Figaro, La serva padrona *and* Tosca.

'Professor Gardini made a great impact on me when I first saw him. It was 1984 at Tokyo Geidai when we were rehearsing Mozart's *Idomeneo*. He was working with the soloists. I was mesmerised by the way he conducted: his expressive use of the baton made it seem part of his body language. With every movement he conveyed the style of the music. I don't think I'd ever seen anyone in Japan conduct in such an artistic way. I decided this was because he was Italian.

'*Maestro*'s Italian-ness has benefited us in many ways. For instance, he has shown us what genuine Italian music is and how to re-create it. Japan is such a long way from Italy that until recently our knowledge of Italian opera was very limited.

'As Japanese musicians, we have a reputation for having good technique, but unfortunately this is often achieved without understanding the spirit of the music. As a result, our playing or singing is often said to lack "soul". I now see that whereas in Japan we start with the technical aspects – which with luck will enable us to achieve the artistic aim – *Maestro* works the other way round. When he's coaching an aria or recitative he talks about the role and what he wants us to produce in terms of meaning, emotion, colour and character. Only after that, and only if necessary, will he discuss technique.

'*Maestro* Gardini's teaching of Italian was a real eye-opener. We Japanese are poor linguists and seeing his coaching I realised that almost all we had learned about the language was wrong. In fact, when we produced the 1992 *Figaro*, it was one of the first occasions in Japan for that opera to be staged in the original language and in an authentic Italian style.

'After his many years spent working with singers of different nationalities, *Maestro* sees diversity as something positive. He never makes us Japanese feel we are different. Rather, he always tries to point out the cultural similarities between Italy and Japan – and there are many. At the same time, he makes it clear that all nationalities are unique.

'Singers and others who have worked with Gardini-*sensei* often comment on how distinctive his productions are. While not everyone he's worked with in Japan is open to his ideas, nonetheless, there are many who do wish to learn how to perform genuine Italian opera. We refer to his way of communicating this as like casting a spell. With an authentic Italian *maestro* in Japan, perhaps we're on the way to achieving an international level in our singing.'

IN CONVERSATION WITH UBALDO GARDINI

IN CONVERSATION WITH UBALDO GARDINI

You have devoted your entire career to working with singers. What is the origin of your fascination with the human voice?

Poetry and song are almost synonymous in classical Italian culture. This is because verse was traditionally recited aloud and when combined with the musicality of our language the effect is of singing. I consider myself lucky to have been surrounded by both arts all my life – initially, within my own family. On a much higher level, Dante's *La divina commedia* contains several references to song – the poet even called his reader *divino cantore* (divine singer) in anticipation of how beautifully the verse would sound.

We Italians regard singing as the purest form of musical expression. We also believe that *la voce è lo specchio dell' anima*, meaning the voice – not the eyes – is the mirror of the soul. So, to be a singer you have to be prepared to express yourself with your whole being. I had no problems persuading musicians to do that in Europe and America – though it was not so easy in Japan.

You mentioned once Lord Byron's description of the Italian language: that it sounds as if it has been written on silk…

Italian, as you know, is very musical and we are rightly proud of our language. The spoken and sung are so intertwined that Puccini's librettist Giuseppe Giacosa said, *Si canta come si parla/Si parla come si canta*, meaning '[If] you sing like you speak, you speak like you sing'.

For opera especially, Italian is a wonderful language. It is expressive, melodic and full of resonant vowels that are helpful for the voice and comfortable to sing. And, phonetically, since most words end in a vowel or contain consonants that function as semi-vowels, they attach themselves easily to each other to create the smooth, beautiful phrases of *bel canto*.

But Italian is also a language in which you must pay attention to every detail. It mostly sounds as it is spelt and depends for its meaning on the accurate pronunciation of vowels, consonants and where the *accento*, here denoting stress, falls. A slip of the tongue and you won't be understood. As a singer, if you mispronounce you're likely to express something quite different – nonsensical, crude even – from what is in the libretto.

What, then, are the main features of Italian pronunciation that a non-Italian singer needs to know?

Let me refer you to Manuel García, whose treatise on singing is an indispensable reference book. He said that to be competent in Italian all that is necessary is a good knowledge of its linguistics, phonetics and speech rhythms. All the artists who worked with me in London and elsewhere know these elements.

One of the most basic things a singer needs to understand is the syllabic nature of the Italian language. Most words fall into three categories. The first type is the *parola tronca*, that is, words of two syllables (sometimes more), in which the stress in on the last, such as '*cantò*', '*mangiò*', '*città*', '*perché*', '*affinchè*', '*ciossiacosà*'. The next is known as *parola sdrucciola*, words of three syllables (sometimes more), in which the stress is on the peri-penultimate, such as '*eccetera*', '*etimologico*', '*operabile*', '*iperbole*'. The largest category is *parola piana*, meaning 'plain' and applied to most regular verbs. In this group, the stress is on the penultimate syllable, for example, '*cantare*', '*centire*', '*vedere*', '*revedere*', '*considerare*'.

It is important for singers to distinguish between these categories because generally, unlike Spanish and other languages with tonic features, there are usually no diacritic markings to help you. This can cause difficulties wherein the slightest shift in stress can create a change of tense or person and make nonsense of what is being sung.

There are other important rules, such as those for accented syllables. For instance, in words of identical spelling, the position of the stress determines the meaning: '*principi*' (pronounced *princIpi*) means 'principles'. But emphasise the first syllable as in '*prIncipi*' and you've got

Yvonne Minton being coached by Ubaldo Gardini for the role of Dorabella in *Così fan tutte*, Royal Opera House Covent Garden

'princes'. Meaning can also change depending on whether the vowels such as [e] and [o] are open or closed. The sharp [s] of '*così*' (as in *Così fan tutte*), if rendered softly as '*cozie*', is meaningless.

I've also heard singers mix up the seemingly innocuous consonants [p] and [b] with embarrassing consequences. When Don Giovanni, with mock concern, in Act I of the opera asks Elvira, 'Che vuoi, mio bene?' (What do you want, my love?), and inadvertently substitutes a [p] for a [b] to sing '*mio pene*', the question becomes narcissistically addressed to his masculinity!

Basic principles such as these are essential for singers learning their roles. For added security and confidence they should speak the libretto – as though in a straight play – *before* they start trying to sing it.

So how can novices achieve a satisfactory level in sung Italian?

First, the good news: you don't necessarily need to be a fluent speaker. If you are competent in three or four roles, you can pick up the rest as you go along. The sung Italian of most of the singers I taught, none of whom initially spoke the language, was impeccable – often better than that of native Italians.

However, after learning the fundamentals of pronunciation, one needs to study with a good Italian coach so as to be able to reproduce the sounds correctly. Thereafter, young singers need an efficient basis for their private study, such as Evelina Colorni's *Singers' Italian, a Manual of Diction and Phonetics,* plus a reputable Italian dictionary containing the International Phonetic Alphabet (IPA) pronunciation symbols. But I have to warn you that a do-it-yourself approach to Italian linguistics can be confusing. Phonetics is not an exact science and you will encounter disagreements between phoneticians, not to mention discrepancies between the IPA symbols and the sounds they represent. That is why a knowledgeable singing teacher or coach is necessary to guide you through.

But first and foremost, singers should ensure they are working from a reliable score – which in the case of Italian opera means the Ricordi edition.

How has Italy's political history had a bearing on the development of the language?

Musicians should not forget that the Italian language derives from Latin. Then they should know that most opera libretti are written in a distinct form, that is, cultured Florentine. From the medieval era until unification of our country in the mid-19th century and the standardisation that came after World War II, every region in Italy had its own separate, local dialect. Because of Florence's literary and artistic importance – Renaissance city, home of artists Michelangelo and Leonardo da Vinci (both of whom, by the way, also wrote poetry), and birthplace of great poets such as Dante, Petrarch and Boccaccio – Florentine Italian was considered the most prestigious. This ensured its later adoption as the basis for the classical, written form. It is no coincidence that Florence is also regarded as the birthplace of opera with the first performance of the Greek-inspired *Dafne* during the sixteenth century.

Most opera libretti are written in verse. What should the singer know about the structure of the text?

As a singer of Italian opera, you are always using poetry. Therefore, you must follow the poetic rules governing the number of syllables and the metre. Recitatives, for example, are usually written in the Italian equivalent of blank verse but the score gives no indication of how to perform them. In that case, one has to sing according to the phrasing in the text – not the beats of the bar. In other words, ignore the bar lines. In fact, Toscanini went further and said, 'Just pronounce the words and you've got the rhythm'.

A good example is Cherubino's and Susanna's 'running duet' in the closet scene in *Le Nozze di Figaro*. Their lines are among the fastest in the operatic repertoire, and therefore, very difficult to get the tongue around. The best way is to speak them first rhythmically. If you go against the natural flow of the language you will have great problems. So will the conductor! I remember one fellow who found it so difficult to conduct this duet that he tried using his metronome. '*Chak-chak-chak-chak-chak-chak-chak-chak*', it went – with the orchestra in fits of laughter. 'Put it away,' I said, 'let me do it.' We succeeded by speaking it – and ensuring the pulse was maintained.

With all these pronunciation rules, how can singers keep their minds clear to concentrate on the pulse?

When you're learning a new piece, the first thing you should do is get a sense of the underlying rhythm. For instance, in 'Porgi amor', the Countess's opening aria, in Act II of *Figaro* (with her plea for the Count to love her again), the syllables and pulse can easily be heard:

Porgi, amor, qualche ristoro
Al mio duolo, a' miei sospir.
O mi rendi il mio tesoro
O mi lascia almen morir.

While you must pay attention to every syllable and know where the liaisons occur – for instance, the [gi] of 'Porgi' joined to the [a] of 'amor' creates the sound [gia] – you would never sing so mechanistically in performance. An important feature of Italian is that the phrases cut naturally across the bar lines. We even have an Italian term for it, '*ritmoide*', that is, a rhythm that ignores them. In other words, the music mustn't sit, it should fly.

Many teachers talk too much about the physiology of singing – the larynx, diaphragm, and so on. But a better way to learn new repertoire is to concentrate on the musical elements. Compared to the aria with its regular rhythm, the recitative, however, causes more difficulties for non-Italians. On their scores, Mozart or Verdi just wrote the instruction, 'sing a recitative', and the Italian singers of the period would have had no difficulty in obliging. If there were any problems, all they had to do was refer to their famous teachers, such as Franscesco Tosi or Giambattista Mancini.

Now that you have alluded to the challenges of the recitative, let's deal with that first. How should singers approach it?

First, they must remember that the recitative is the most important element of the libretto. (I'm still astonished sometimes, admittedly mainly in Asia, when I find that musicians and academics, who should know better, regard the recitatives as mere fillers between arias. I even worked with one opera company where the producer wanted to omit them altogether!) The recitative is crucial to the opera, especially because it has the same function as the dialogue in a play, allowing the story to unfold and bringing the characters to life.

Anyone can sing an aria. But an engaging performance of the recitative is what marks out singers with the potential to attain international level. Sung with the natural phrasing of speech and almost *a capella* [accompanied by only the occasional chord on the harpsichord], it exposes not only their competence with the Italian language but also their acting ability. During the preparation of an opera, I've found that when singers get the recitative right, after that everything else is easy.

So how can they sing the recitative confidently and convincingly?

Once the words and music are learnt, the artists should forget the bar lines and concentrate on the flow of the natural speech. (We say '*non quadrato*', that is, not to sing it in regular beats.) They must also be prepared for 'oddities' such as the main accent occurring in an unmusical place, like the middle of a bar. For ensemble recitatives, the characters' lines must dovetail into each other, even though rests may be marked on the score.

To get the recitative dramatically right, the pace of the lines must be varied to do justice not only to the plot but also to the sub-text and the characterisation. So, *per esempio*, in the opening scene of *Figaro* where our hero is measuring the room for himself and his future bride, Susanna sings, 'Cosa stai misurando/Caro il mio Figaretto?' (What are you measuring, my little Figaro?) He replies, 'Io guardo se quell letto/Che ci destina il Conte /Farà buona figura in questo loco.' (I'm trying to see the best place for the bed that the Count has given us.) Susanna retorts, 'E in questa stanza?' (And in this room?) He continues, 'Certo: a noi la cede/Generoso il padrone.' (Certainly, our lord has generously given it [the bed] to us.) Susanna's lines should be paced differently from Figaro's to suggest, among other things, her incredulity at his naïve acceptance of the Count's 'gift'. From that little example you can see how a recitative, sung dramatically, can set the whole scene. But to achieve that level of subtlety and nuance you need a knowledgeable director along with committed and talented artists prepared for endless rehearsing.

Several directors were impressed by how you always emphasised the drama of the operas. How important is the libretto compared with the music?

I like to think of opera as music-drama and regard the librettist as a dramatist and the composer his collaborator. And don't forget that Wagner believed music's function is, by turn, to convey, express and reinforce the poetry, tragedy or comedy that is the basis of the opera. He talked about the music 'driving home' what's in the libretto.

Ubaldo Gardini in discussion with Ruggero Raimondi, who is renowned for his performances as Don Giovanni

Beautiful words make beautiful operas and it is the partnership between composers and their librettists that is the key to success. When Da Ponte handed Mozart a libretto he gave him, at the same time, the rhythm of the arias. Take *Figaro* again. After reading 'Voi che sapete/Che cosa è amor/Donne, vedete/S'io l'ho nel cor', and so on, all Mozart had to do was write the tune. The rhythm was there already in the text. No composer, no matter how great, could alter it.

Much of the fame of the best composers of Italian opera is in no small measure due to their librettists. It is no coincidence that the texts for Mozart's three most accomplished operas (*Figaro, Così* and *Don Giovanni*) were all written by the greatest dramatic poet, Da Ponte. Puccini – another notable Tuscan and exponent of *la parola regna suprema* – based his greatest operas, *La Bohème, Tosca* and *Madama Butterfly,* on libretti by Giuseppe Giacosa. Verdi, too, said, 'Through the words I find the right tempo, melody – everything'.

How did you get your singers to learn the libretto?

First, singers must remember that they are really actors and what they are singing is a kind of heightened sung-speech in which every word and idea is important. That is why I am so against training singers by *solfège* or wordless exercises. Drills such as these can prevent singers from appreciating the importance of language and how to deal with it – for instance, how to express emotion and articulate clearly.

So, the first step is to have a word-by-word understanding of what you are singing. If you then recite the lines aloud rhythmically, the breathing will be right, and when you start to sing, you'll get the best out of your voice.

To familiarise my singers with the libretto, I would firstly get them to speak the lines in a comfortable region of the voice. Then we would go to the music and put the two together. The principle of the great, old Italian schools of the past was to sing on the words! That means you have to colour each one differently.

I also believe that you must know the text and music thoroughly *before* the ensemble rehearsals. Giuseppe Di Stefano used to complain that Herbert von Karajan always wanted his cast to move onto the stage too soon, that is, before they were completely at home in their singing roles. If the poetry and the music are not firmly in place and the singing is under-confident, the stagework will suffer.

Do any particularly humorous gaffes come to mind through singers not understanding the libretto?

Many. But there is one in particular that never ceases to amuse me when I think back on it. It occurred in a *Tosca* in the chapel scene at the end of Act I when Scarpia, having succeeded in making Tosca jealous, should sing, 'Già il veleno, l'ha rosa' (meaning, 'my poison eats into her', but literally, 'already the poison has corroded her'). However, in the mistaken belief that the line was about bringing a rose to Tosca, Scarpia came on stage bearing the said flower – to the utter bafflement of the audience.

Even simple mispronunciations can change meaning – with comic results. There is one example from Act II of *La Traviata*, when Germont, the father of Alfredo, meeting Violetta for the first time complains how his son has been 'bewitched by you'. Instead of the phrase 'ammaliato da voi,' that particular Germont sang it as '*ammagliato* da voi'. The subtle addition of the [gl] consonant, with its connotation of 'to knit', suggested to knowing Italian ears a nonsensical allusion to thick underwear.

Let's assume that the soloists understand what they're singing, can you remind us of some essential pronunciation rules? Let's start with the Italian vowels, and can you provide some English equivalences?

I cannot provide a definitive guide to Italian pronunciation for Anglo-Saxons. One reason is that Italian has several sounds that don't exist in standard English, for instance the closed [e] and [o]. So I have to caution that the English equivalences below are, in many cases, approximations.

For the purposes of singing, I concentrate on seven main vowel sounds. They are:

[i] Italian: *tipi/silenzio/finestra*; as in English m**ea**n/s**ee**/**ea**se

[e] (Closed) Italian: *Verdi/stella/vede*; as in English **eh**/b**a**ke/c**a**ke (with a Northern English accent)

[ɛ] (Open) Italian: *certo/lento/bello*; as in English m**e**t/s**e**t/**e**gg

[a] Italian: *marco/patria/caro*; as in English: l**a**ss/b**a**ck/m**a**t

[ɔ] (Open) Italian: *rosa/poco/morte*; as in English c**o**rn/Southern English RP c**au**ght/ Scottish h**o**t

[o] (Closed) Italian: *dolce/molto/voce*; as in English **o**h/h**o**me/c**o**mb (with a Northern English accent)

[u] Italian: *luna/busto/funghi*; as in English wh**o**m/b**oo**m/l**u**te

Depending on their position in a word, the vowels can be short or long, the latter recognisable by the phonetic symbol [:]. For instance, *'v[i]tto'* (food) has a short [i], whereas *'v[i:]no'* (wine) is long. Similarly, *'c[o]rto'* (brief) has a short [o] as opposed to *'c[o:]me'* (how).

Because the position of the tongue – its height and the area that is raised or lowered – determines how these vowels are produced, familiarisation with the triangle of cardinal vowels, reproduced in most books on phonetics and linguistics, can be helpful.

Getting to grips with the vowels seems fairly simple and straightforward. Is it?

No, Anglo-Saxons have several problems with vowels. The first essential is to learn to sing them without an English diphthong. Think of each vowel as a square of marble. When you sing *amore*, the final [e] should be sung as it is written and not like '*amorei*'. The effect of a diphthong is like sliding the bow on the violin. For a singer it's not good and can cause mistakes in meaning.

I remember once in *La Bohème* where Mimi wants to declare her love to Rodolfo in the following, 'Ho tante cose che ti voglio dire /O una sola, ma grande come il mare/Come il mare profunda ed infinita/Sei il mio amor...' (I've so many things that I want to say to you/or one alone, but big as the sea/Like the sea deep and infinite/You are my love.) In short, 'I've so many things that I want to say to you... but the main one (*una sola*) is that I love you.' However, instead of 'sola', Mimi inserted a diphthong and sang '*suola*', meaning the sole of her shoe – thereby reducing the declaration to the nonsensical 'I've got a shoe as wide as the ocean'.

Yet another bad habit is the insertion of a kind of [y] in the middle of two consecutive vowels, making, for instance, *'mie'* sound like *mi-ye*. Words such as *'viene'*, *'cuore'*, *'suore'* must be sung cleanly cut, as [vi-ene], [cu-ore], [su-ore]. People also tend to put that intrusive [y] even before the initial vowel in a word. I used to hear the best example of that over the PA system at Covent Garden. My name would be announced as 'Yubaldo' Gardini. To preserve my sanity *[laughing]* I told them just to call me 'U.G'. But that didn't solve the problem either. I became '*Yu G*'.

The Italian consonants can also be very difficult for Anglo-Saxons. Can you give us some guidance, firstly on those at the beginning of words? I'm thinking of the [d] and [t] or [p] and [b] sounds which are so different in Italian.

Generally speaking, these initial consonants are softer and less plosive than their English counterparts. By that I mean, less air is required to articulate them. The singer must be aware not only of the difference but also of which vocal organs to use. Take the words *'treno'* and its English equivalent 'train'. To produce the English [t], the tip of the tongue is raised to touch the hard palate just behind the upper front teeth and then released. But for the Italian *'treno'*, the tongue moves a fraction forward to touch behind the upper front teeth while the air expelled is minimal. The Italian word *'donna'*, mistakenly articulated with an English [d] as in the English verb 'done', is another example. The same goes for words that commence with the Italian [p] and [b]. The [p] of *'pace'* is not as explosive as its English equivalent 'peace'.

Sometimes in our fear of over-articulating these initial consonants, we almost avoid them altogether and go straight to the vowel. Do you have any advice on how to sing them correctly?

While vowels must be given full vocal tone, the consonants are also important. Even though the Italian versions are generally softer and less sharp than English, we still need to sing them! The attractiveness of the Italian syllable derives from the combination of consonant and vowel – and from that, the rhythm of the poetry. We also say *'nel connubio'* to describe the power that comes from the marriage between the syllables and the music. When the artists get the syllables right, they'll have no difficulty pronouncing the words correctly.

Ubaldo Gardini coaching at Covent Garden from his heavily marked score

There is a simple technique to ensure that consonants at the beginning of words are heard. That is, they must be sung before the note value. Then the adjoining vowels will be in tempo. Particularly difficult are the closed consonants such as the [c], [t] or [p] – for example in *Figaro*, the [c] of 'Caro mio ben', the [t] of 'Tippe tappe', the

[p] of 'Porgi amor'. The composer cannot anticipate the consonants – but that's how they should be sung. Indeed, the only way to be heard in the theatre is to over-enunciate them. When you do this you can become the greatest actor with your voice.

What about consonants in the middle of words?

A word that is often sung wrongly not just by the soloist but the whole chorus is the 'evviva' ('hurrah') for the Count at the end of Act I in *Figaro*. I've heard the word rendered as '*Eviva... eviva ... eviva*', as though there was only one, barely audible [v]. But it's not that. It's pronounced '*Eev-v-iva...Eev-v-iva ... Eev-v-iva*'. In other words, each [v] must be articulated clearly.

Can you say something about the double consonants that don't exist in English and are so difficult to get right?

We have many words with double consonants. Phonetically, they take longer to pronounce than corresponding single consonants and must be expressed strongly and clearly. The syllables are usually separated – and the first is longer than the second. (In the dictionary they are indicated by the central colon, for example, '*tut:to*', '*bel:lo*', '*an:no*'.) The tongue remains in position after the first consonant of the pair, before being released to articulate the second.

Mistakes with double consonants are legion – for instance when the artist sings a single consonant instead of a double. *Per esempio*, '*donna*' (pronounced *don:na* and meaning 'woman' as in 'La donna è mobile') if sung as though there's only one [n] sound becomes '*dona*', meaning 'give', and obviously destroys the sense. Another example, resulting in absurdity, often occurs in *Don Pasquale*. Dottore Malatesta, who should precede the list of qualities in the bride he has found for his nephew Pasquale with 'Bella [*bel:la*] siccome un angelo' (lovely as an angel), has occasionally ruined the romantic simile by dropping an [l] so the word becomes '*bela*' – thereby suggesting that 'she bleats like an angel'.

You once said how mistakes can also occur when singers inadvertently insert extra consonants or vowels not in the text.

This can also cause problems. One among the many I've heard occurs at the beginning of *Madama Butterfly* where Pinkerton is describing to Sharpless the little house ('una casetta') he has just bought for himself and his new bride. However, if he inserts an extra [s] to make it *'cassetta'*, [*cas:seta*], the house diminutively reduces to a box! I also once heard Tosca tell Cavaradossi not to 'sigh for our box' when instead of 'non la sospiri la nostra casetta,' he mistakenly sang 'la nostra *cassetta*'.

Another example, with hilarious results, comes to mind where what should have been a single consonant was altered to a double. This occurred in the recitative in *Don Giovanni* where an incredulous Don Ottavio declares his intention to investigate Don Giovanni's alleged exploits. In vowing to spare no effort to learn the truth, the tenor should sing, '...Ah di scoprire il vero' (until I find where the truth lies.) However, instead, he sang *'il verro'* [*ver:ro*], creating the puzzling phrase, 'until I find where the boar lies'.

Are there any other consonant rules that the singer is expected to know that are not indicated in the score?

There are many. But let's finally look at what we call syntactic doubling, in Italian known as *'raddoppiamento sintattico'* – when a consonant is doubled because of the vowel-ending of the previous word, like *'così'*. So 'così fan tutte' for example, is sung as *'così [f]fan tutte.'* Likewise, 'è mio', is rendered as *'è[m]mìo'*. The same rules apply to the words following 'ove' and 'dove' and others. So, in 'Dove sono i bei momenti' from *Figaro*, 'Dove sono' is sung as *'Dove [s]sono'*. You have to be careful to articulate the syllables clearly and not slide them into each other.

Then there are consonants, which because of the way they are sung, function as *semi-vocale* or semi-vowels. These are [l], [m], [n], [r] – along with the [s] of Latin words. When we sing these consonants we must elongate them and make the succeeding syllable softer and shorter. *Per esempio*, in a word like *'alto'*, we sing through the word prolonging the [l] of the first syllable and then softening the second so that it sounds like [allto]. Similarly, *'antro'* becomes [anntro], *'antico'*,[anntico], *'cantare'*, [cantarre], *'cantiamo'*, [cantiammo], *'cantalo'*, [cantallo], and so on.

You told me how when the Royal Opera House Covent Garden performed once at La Scala the Italian critics commented on the standard of their Italian. How did you achieve such a high level?

My way of preparing the singers was like this. I would start with the Italian phonetics. We might spend a week on them, repeating and repeating until everyone got the correct pronunciation. Then and only then would we move on to working with the *répétiteur*. The singers who were hardest to work with were those with some – often faulty – knowledge of the Italian language. In that case, we would have to go back to basics and unlearn the bad, old habits. It was easier to start with those who knew no Italian at all.

From left: Monserrat Caballé, José Carreras, conductor Jesús López-Cobos and producer Erik Smith during the 1976 recording of *Lucia de Lammermoor* which was coached by Ubaldo Gardini

I expected everyone to produce their best efforts and aim for perfect pronunciation. If it was less than one hundred percent I would consider the result mediocre. 'You'll never become world-class performers if you're just average,' I would tell these singers. The truly talented responded and pushed themselves to give their all. The result is that so many of the artists I trained have gone on to have international careers – and in Britain even had their talents recognised by honours from the Queen.

Many interviewees have remarked on the helpfulness of the analogies you drew with the smooth line produced by the violin.

It's to do with the bowing, the *cavata*. In Italian when we say a violinist has a powerful *cavata* that means they are able to pull out from themselves the most beautiful, possible sound. You must also do that with singing – and like changing the bowing without stoppage, you mustn't break the vocal line. If you get the right tone, that is the truest singing technique. The advice of Gemiani, the famous violinist, to 'never play a note without meaning', also applies to singing. He further commented that the greatest violinist is the one who resembles an orator. Indeed, that's how I would describe great vocal artists – singing like orators to theatres of several thousands.

Surely to sing like an orator requires a big voice. How can singers produce the volume necessary for opera? First, how about the breathing?

Before we start to sing, we Italians just mentally say *ispirare*, meaning 'inspire yourself'. In other words, while you're taking that first breath, think ahead to the sense of what you're going to sing. Get into the spirit of the piece. Otherwise, breathing becomes a mere physiological action. You must forget about the diaphragm – and just breathe naturally and sing. That way you avoid the contortions that can result from over-emphasis on mechanics and technique.

The greatest singer is the one with the best breath control. As I said, Italian is one of the world's easiest languages to sing, the soft consonants and rich vowels ensuring that the notes and words flow easily into each other in a continuous line of sound. In English, on the other hand, the diphthongs and aspirated consonants use up more air and require greater technique. With its minimal loss of breath, you could say Italian sings itself.

Many singing teachers offer conflicting advice on where to breathe before starting to sing. Some say breathe deeply before the phrase, others recommend the upbeat, yet others to snatch a quick breath. Where is the best place?

The breath gives life to the music. After that you need a lot of strength to use it efficiently. The first breath should always be taken on the beat before starting to sing. Let's take Don Ottavio's recitative from *Don Giovanni* which he sings after Donna Anna's assertions about the villain's [Don Giovanni's] attack on both herself and her father. He pledges either to disprove them or seek vengeance. The breathing is usually as follows:

√ 'Come mai creder deggio
Di sì nero delitto
Capace un cavaliero! √
Ah, di scopire il vero
Ogni mezzo si cerchi! √ Io sento in petto
E di sposo e d'amico √
Il dover che mi parla: √
Disingannarla voglio, o vendicarla.'

(Literally translated, this reads:
How can I ever believe a cavalier capable of such a black crime?
Ah, I will use every means to discover the truth.
I feel in my breast, both as her [Anna's] betrothed and friend,
The duty which speaks to me:
I wish to undeceive her or avenge her.)

However, because this is a recitative, the tenor can take it at his own comfortable pace.

I cannot emphasise enough how the body is the most perfect mechanism if left to do things naturally. The bizarre exercises for the voice and the diaphragm that some teachers insist on are a deterrent to true vocal expression. Singers must try to find their own voice and sing freely. Many of the most famous artists started out with no formal training at all. José Carreras told me that his dentist taught him how to sing. Plácido Domingo, from his boyhood, sang with his parents in the Zarzuela opera in Spain – without a singing teacher. Carlo Bergonzi had only one lesson in which his *professore* tried to turn him into a baritone. After that he taught himself.

To fill the vast space of the opera house consumes a lot of breath. What is the best technique for amplifying the sound?

The best way to achieve volume is to use the resonance of the hard palate. If you open the mouth too wide the tone becomes uneven. The sound must also be intense and controlled and should never shake or wobble.

Several singers attribute their ability to sing bel canto *from you. How would you define it and how it is produced?*

The term *bel canto* means no more than beautiful singing. It's as though the singer is just singing one long note, flying above the orchestra. One thing you have to remember is that Italian singing is always *legato* – even if the composer hasn't written that performance direction. Otherwise it is not Italian. But nowadays people often interpret *bel canto* as a chance to shout and it becomes 'can belto'! [*laughing*]. This is true especially in Japan. Operatic singing is not about loudness. The hardest thing is to sing *piano*, and *pp* even more so. Many of the artists I coached could captivate their audiences with the most beautiful and intense *pianissimos*.

The singers who worked with you are renowned not only for their accurate pronunciation but also for their good diction. Gwynne Howell told me that this was one of the most important things he learned from you. How did you train the singers to enunciate distinctly?

Good diction is dependent on being able to sing a long line without running out of breath. Where there is no unnecessary expenditure of air, intensity will be maintained and the diction will be clear. At first, Gwynne was surprised at the long phrases I demanded from him but he has a great emotional range and was eager to learn.

But for the audience to hear and understand every word also involves projection. The singer needs to look as far out into the auditorium as possible – because the voice goes as far as the eyes – and you have to be in control of the sound. It can be a small sound that goes back into the theatre and becomes bigger and bigger. You have to use all the resonance possible – and remember the principle that with the least effort comes the greatest result.

Singers and conductors have mentioned the excellent ear training you provided in teaching them how to listen.

It is difficult for singers to hear their own voices. It needs others – music coaches and especially the conductor – to ensure the tuning is right, and if not, to advise on what to do. But singers must also listen intently to each other. Because the piano is a 'tempered' instrument, with a fixed pitch, it is out of tune compared to the human voice, which, like a stringed instrument, sings on a natural scale. So for rehearsals, the piano should always be toned down in order not to distort the natural harmonics of the voice.

Several of your artists told me one of your great skills was in getting established singers to take risks, to go beyond what they think is their limit in order to find their true potential.

A great singer like Janet Baker could do anything. But she needed another Janet Baker, who was external, to push her. 'Don't take a breath, go beyond, go on,' I would urge her. It's what the French call *technique supérieure*, a technique that is beyond technique. You leave the ground. It's like mind over matter.

But in the final analysis, remember that the singing coach is not employed to teach the basics of operatic art. We are there to equip singers to cope with any role, after which you are ready to fly. In Italy you reach a certain point and then your *professore* says, "You don't need me anymore. You've learned all I can teach you. Now you're on your own. Just come back sometime and perform for me". I would merely add that once you have learnt the principles and techniques of singing in Italian, you can apply them to any language.

Richard van Allan as the Don with Alan Opie as Sancho Panza in *Don Quichotte* at English National Opera

MEET THE ARTISTS

Biographies & Interviews Part Three

...in the title role, *La Fille du Régiment*, Tiroler Landestheater Innsbruck

Gaining first prize in the Australian Singing Competition marked the beginning of an international career for Vienna-based Japanese soprano, **Akiko Nakajima**. Several debuts soon followed, including *La clemenza di Tito* (Opera Australia), *La Bohème* (Teatro di San Carlo Naples), and a prize-winning performance in the title role of *Alcina* (Innsbruck's Festwochen der Alten Musik). She sang principal roles with both the Tiroler Landestheater Innsbruck and the Staatstheater Darmstadt. Her appearances as Adina (*L'elisir d'amore*), Amina (*La sonnambula*) and Marie (*La Fille du Régiment*) were greeted with great acclaim, while her triumph as Lucia di Lammermoor led to her nomination as the best singer of the year (1998) by *Opernwelt* magazine.

Miss Nakajima's 1999 debut at the Vienna Volksoper as Sonja in *Der Zarewitsch* was followed by other successes including Violetta (*La Traviata*) and Anne Trulove (*The Rake's Progress*). She has sung the role of Fiorilla in *Il Turco in Italia* at the Royal Opera House Covent Garden and, most recently, for Hamburg Staatsoper. Among the numerous conductors with whom she has worked are: Lorin Maazel, Herbert Blomstedt, Charles Dutoit, Kazushi Ono, Myung-Whun Chung and Thomas Hengelbrock. Her broad repertoire has taken her to some of Europe's most prestigious concert halls and helped her to build up an impressive discography. Her career has also continued to develop in Japan where she regularly performs with the NHK Symphony Orchestra and at the New National Theatre of Japan, Tokyo.

Akiko Nakajima was coached by Ubaldo Gardini for several roles, most notably, Violetta (La Traviata).

'When Ubaldo was working in Vienna he would often call me up suddenly and announce, "I know it's Sunday but it's a lovely day. Come for a walk and afterwards I'll give you a singing lesson". And that's what we'd do. Aside from our lessons, we had great conversations about *Madama Butterfly* (it was just after the Geidai/San Francisco joint production in Japan), other operas, singing, composers – all sorts of musical topics. Now nearly a decade later, I look back nostalgically on that stimulating period.

'I have been studying with Ubaldo for many years and regard him as inspiring. It is difficult to compare him with other coaches. He is a great musician and artist with whom you can relate on many levels, not only singing but everything operatic, from accompanying to conducting. Without him there's no doubt that my career wouldn't have happened.

'Ubaldo's way of working is unique. He not only conducts in front of you, but he is also physically and spiritually involved. He is breathing and singing along with you – often so much that you don't know if *you're* singing or not, and when a difficult phrase comes, he sort of makes this crazy noise, often so loud that you can't hear yourself. But you're not afraid. Then somehow it passes. Other times he doesn't have to do anything, because intuitively you sense beforehand what he will say. It is difficult to describe the magic, the madness that is happening when Ubaldo is coaching and someone like Nils Muss is accompanying.

'Occasionally I feel as if my spirit is flying away. I'm so lost in the role that I don't know if I'm singing anymore and I only look at Ubaldo when I need to. Other times when I'm exhausted, he will work with the pianist on some phrasing in the score. This gives me time to rethink, make some notes, or just revert to controlled breathing. Then when he thinks I'm ready he'll turn his attention back to me. He won't say beforehand, "OK, you've had enough, take a little break, then we'll do such and such". He just switches. It's a trick, I'm used to it now.

'Many facets of his teaching will remain with me forever. "If you look beautiful, you will sing beautifully," he would say, "because the face is the mirror of the soul. If you twist your face, that's because you are twisted in your singing." He also encouraged me to have my own interpretation of a character, and where I express emotion to ensure that it is sincerely felt: "You may be criticised, but you must have your own way of doing things." He knows me very well and also how I can introduce a flirtatious element into a role. "Use it, don't hide it," he suggested.

'Ubaldo also advised me never to dictate to a conductor. "Give him the feeling that he can trust you, then you are free. Don't reveal all your secrets, your slightly different rhythms. Swim in the music, and give him what he needs so that he is secure." So I say to the conductor, "Here, I'll sing a looser rhythm, but keep it going. I will meet you in the pause."

'I suppose that everything Ubaldo has taught me can be summed up in the philosophy that, as a singer I am not on stage to slavishly follow notes in a score. Rather, I am an interpretative artist who through my singing and acting has to convey both my character's emotions and psychological truth.'

JESSYE NORMAN
SOPRANO

...as Ariadne, *Ariadne auf Naxos*, The Royal Opera House Covent Garden

Jessye Norman is 'one of those once-in-a-generation singers who is not simply following in the footsteps of others, but is staking out her own niche in the history of singing'. This rich history continues to be made as she brings her sumptuous sound, her joy of singing and spontaneous passion to recital performances, operatic portrayals and appearances with symphony orchestras and chamber music collaborators to audiences around the world. The sheer size, power, and lustre of her voice share equal acclaim with her thoughtful music-making, innovative programming of the classics, and fervent advocacy of contemporary music. Miss Norman's innovative collaborations with artists on the cutting-edge in their fields, such as Robert Wilson, André Heller, Bill T. Jones and Steve McQueen, serve to add new dimensions and exciting new challenges to her work.

Miss Norman is the recipient of many awards and honors. In December of 1997, she was invested with the United States' highest award in the performing arts, the Kennedy Center Honor, making history as the youngest recipient in its twenty-year existence. Her many other distinctions include honorary doctorates at some thirty colleges, universities and conservatories around the world. An orchid has been named for her by the Museum of Natural History in France, and in 1984 the French government bestowed upon Miss Norman the title *Commandeur de L'Ordre des Arts et des Lettres*. She was awarded *Le Légion d'Honneur* by the French president, François Mitterand, in 1989. Miss Norman's Fourth Grammy, The Lifetime Achievement Award for Classical Music, was presented in 2006.

[from Jessye Norman's current concert programme.]

Ubaldo Gardini prepared Jessye Norman for the following recordings: Giulietta (Un giorno di regno), *Medora* (Il corsaro), *both conducted by Lamberto Gardelli; the Countess* (Le Nozze di Figaro) *and Idamante* (Idomeneo) *under Sir Colin Davis. She also worked with Maestro Gardini for performances of* Idomeneo *at the Rome Opera.*

'I was privileged to have first worked with Ubaldo Gardini in the early 1970s at the time of my initial collaborations with Sir Colin Davis.

'I apply Ubaldo's vision of sung Italian every time I perform – whether in Italian or any other language. His special strength – and I am not comparing him to anyone as this is totally unnecessary – lies in his ability to remain absolutely committed to listening to every single word. We weren't allowed lazy "*r's*" or to skip over double consonants. For their part, Italian singers had to get rid of their regional accents. He represented total commitment and expected it of us, too.

'Ubaldo does have a wonderful chemistry with singers since he understands the tensions that can develop while preparing for a performance. He would always begin his sentence with something like "A cara mia, un momento, per favore!" and the correction would follow in the most helpful and exacting but gentle way. He knows that his work is essential to the whole. Yet he never imposed himself, only his vast knowledge.

'He possesses a brilliant understanding of the *legato* line and how the art of the *cantabile* is the root of all good singing. High on the list of the things I learned is the importance of allowing Italian to move freely over the tongue, out of the mouth and supported by an understanding of the beauty of pure vowels and the thrust of the consonants. No clenched jaws, no tight throats, no closed anything – in other words, freedom. The anatomy of singing is as important a field of study as the technical aspects of producing an agreeable sound.

'The powerful instruction of someone of Ubaldo Gardini's talent is needed more than ever in today's hectic, anxious-to-perform atmosphere. But a well-rounded, prepared performer is always more interesting. A curious mind is important in any field, especially in the performing arts. Nowadays, many schools are failing in their preparation of young singers. For example, the study of language is often not required, and the vocal pedagogue, the truly knowledgeable singing expert, is becoming a rarity.

'I am one of Ubaldo's fans. He has always been a wonderful support and marvellous cheerleader. He is a great man. I was always happy to have his comforting presence and his well-considered instruction and counsel.'

YASUHIKO OKUHATA
LIGHTING DESIGNER

One of Ubaldo Gardini's longest-serving artistic collaborators, **Yasuhiko Okuhata** works as a lighting designer for opera, theatre, dance and ballet. After enrolling on a sociology programme at Hosei University, Tokyo, his interest in drama and the arts took over and he left to embark on a course in stage arts and lighting. A subsequent Japanese Ministry of Culture scholarship won him a year's study in Europe. His operatic work has been recognised by the Japanese Lighting Designers' Association among others, with awards for such productions as: Puccini's *Trittico* (1983), *Maria Stuarda* (1985) and *Otello* (1992).

Mr Okuhata's international experience includes lighting operas in New York, Warsaw, Taiwan and Hong Kong. He has also been engaged to work for companies such as the Netherlands Dance Theatre and Cologne Opera.

Yasuhiko Okuhata's lighting credits with Ubaldo Gardini include: Idomeneo *and* Le Nozze di Figaro *(both at Tokyo Geidai University of the Arts) and* Don Giovanni *(Tokyo Music College). He also lit the 2007* Le Nozze di Figaro, *directed by Maestro Gardini, to celebrate the centenary of Tokyo Music College.*

'We stage Western opera in Japan under difficult conditions. No domestic opera company has its own permanent performance space. Instead, we rent out venues for a two- or three-night run, with limited time, budget, facilities and backstage staff. The equipment can be very primitive. Compared to Europe, here the lighting is one of the last artistic elements of a production to be considered.

'We are still influenced by our Japanese traditions. So, for example, stage lighting has always been simple and two-dimensional. In *kabuki* theatre depth is suggested by colourful costumes and stage sets. Thus, the lighting is either on or off – its objective being to show up the vividly painted faces of the actors who deliver their lines close to the audience. So, while Japan is said to have invented stage lighting in the 17th century using candles in front of these actors, we have had no significant developments since.

'During my visit to Europe in 1984, observing different theatre productions, I saw how Western lighting designers are considered part of the creative team and often involved all through the rehearsal process. They can use an enormous range of equipment to provide colour, or to suggest such elements as the setting, atmosphere, drama or psychological states – and to light up the faces of the singers who are upstage away from the audience.

'When I first met *Maestro* Gardini it was for a Tokyo Geidai production of *Idomeneo*. I was particularly impressed by his architectural approach to the staging, that is, the cast's use of the whole stage space. Despite the limitations of lighting in the opera world here, I try to fit in with *Maestro*'s artistic concept, be creative and make my designs as beautiful and authentic as possible. I cannot help thinking that if conditions were more like those in Europe, working with *Maestro* Gardini we could certainly achieve some remarkable productions, unique to our domestic opera scene.'

KATHERINE OLSEN

ACCOMPANIST, COACH & ARTISTS' MANAGER

Katherine M. Olsen, founder of Encompass Arts Management LLC, whose roster includes Cheryl Studer and Marcello Giordani, is one of the most sought after coach-accompanists in the American music world. She holds a Bachelor's and a Master's Degree in Piano Performance from the University of Tennessee. After leaving her position as coach at the Juilliard School of Music she was engaged by the Lyric Opera of Chicago.

With her sound musicianship and foreign language skills, Miss Olson works with Broadway and film artists (including Faye Dunaway), along with renowned opera singers such as Ben Heppner, Deborah Voigt, Sherrill Milnes, Gary Lakes and Martina Arroyo. She is also Artistic Administrator for the Music Department of Baz Luhrmann's Tony Award-winning Broadway production of *La Bohème*.

A frequent pianist for prestigious music competitions, Katherine Olsen has played for the Richard Tucker Foundation, the George London Foundation, Voci Verdiane in Busseto, Italy, The Heinz Refuss Competition, The Belvedere Competition and the Deutsche Oper Berlin Foundation. She has also conducted an original musical called *Buster Drumright*, starring two-time Tony award winner, John Cullum.

Katherine Olson played the piano for all or part of the following operas coached by Ubaldo Gardini at the Juilliard School of Music, New York: La Traviata, I Cappelletti I Montecchi, Lucia di Lammermoor *and* Tosca.

'As both accompanist and coach, I use what I learned from Ubaldo every day. I first met him when I was at Juilliard in the early 1980s. I was hired by the renowned head coach, Martin Smith, to play and coach the operas. Among the students were Renée Fleming and Hei-Kyung Hong. When *Maestro* Gardini came into the picture, they said perhaps I'd like to accompany his vocal classes. Because he had an Italian name, I thought, "I'm going to jump at this opportunity".

'Even though I hadn't had much experience of other coaches, I think I knew at the time, despite being so young, that with his unique approach and attention to detail, there was no one like him. To this day, I can still hear his singing voice, even though it was not particularly beautiful. As the pianist, I could tell exactly what he wanted his students to do – and, on the whole, so could they. They were young voices, yet he seemed to work miracles with them. Of course, there were others, too, who just wanted to run through the music because their attitude was, "I'm already at the Metropolitan Opera, what can this person teach me?".

'His unique approach to opera preparation particularly inspired and excited me. *Maestro*'s favourite word was "*ancore*" because you did everything again and again and again. We did a lot of work in the *bel canto* style, because opera *verismo* was obviously his thing. On these occasions he would often concentrate on the accompanist. He would work with me to find the underpinning and the drama in the orchestral score, which I then had to reproduce as my own piano reduction. Just playing the notes is good enough for some coaches, but not Ubaldo. He showed us that the accompanist had to go beyond that to become, in effect a miniature orchestra. Then when the singers start working with the full instrumental ensemble they will be already familiar with the various elements and textures in the score, from which to find their own notes and tonality.

'An important element of his teaching was ear training. When he ran over time, he'd bring the next singer in to listen to the one having the lesson. You could learn a lot this way. Other pianists were encouraged to observe his classes.

'Even if Ubaldo came back on the international scene today, I think he would be exceptional, because we're really talking about tradition, that link to the past. He knew the style of operas along with their performance history. Nowadays, a lot of the coaching and the musical preparation is like American fast food. Things are approximated and it becomes a case of "let's get through everything as quickly as we can". Back then, we had time.'

KAZUSHI ONO

CONDUCTOR

...with the BBC National Orchestra of Wales, St David's Hall Cardiff, 2006

Kazushi Ono was born in Tokyo and is a graduate of the conducting department of Geidai University of the Arts. Prior to becoming Music Director of Théâtre de la Monnaie Brussels in 2002 (succeeding Antonio Pappano), he conducted the Tokyo Philharmonic Orchestra for concerts and productions by the Nikikai Opera Company.

His debut at La Monnaie (Richard Strauss's *Elektra*) was described by the *Suddeutsche Zeitung* as 'the miracle of Brussels'. Since then, critically acclaimed productions have included *Boris Godunov, Don Giovanni, Peter Grimes, Tannhäuser, Der Fliegende Holländer, Aïda, Falstaff* and *Die Frau ohne Schatten*. He has also conducted several world premieres, including *Julie* by Philippe Boesmans. In autumn 2005 Kazushi Ono and La Monnaie made their first Japanese tour with *Don Giovanni* and two orchestral programmes.

Mr Ono works regularly with several of the world's leading orchestras. His debut at La Scala Milan (initially with a symphonic repertoire) was followed by *Lady Macbeth of Mtsensk*. In 2006 he made his debut at the BBC Proms in London with the BBC National Orchestra of Wales.

After his final season as Musical Director at La Monnaie, Mr Ono's burgeoning international career is taking him to conduct at the Metropolitan Opera House New York, the Paris Opéra, Glyndebourne and La Scala Milan. Several important orchestral concerts are also scheduled.

Kazushi Ono frequently returns to conduct in Japan where his success has been recognised with many prizes including the Idemitsu, Hideo Saito and the Japanese Ministry of Culture Arts Awards.

The operas on which Kazushi Ono worked with Ubaldo Gardini include: Rigoletto (*Kansai Nikikai*), Madama Butterfly, La Bohème *and* Turandot (*all Tokyo Nikikai*).

'Much of my knowledge of Italian opera is attributable to Ubaldo Gardini – especially the need for authenticity and an individual approach. As a result, I am quite proud of the standard of my productions.

'As part of my preparation, I used to go to his home with a pianist, taking my score and libretto. His music room is full of books, including different versions of the score, volumes for background reading, and letters of the composers. He'd rifle through them excitedly and pull out the relevant volume to illustrate some points about an opera's creator or its cultural background. He has so much knowledge that I regard him as a kind of medium in contact with composers.

'While I would shape the opera externally, he would guide me on the other elements. He would also go into detail about the layers of meaning underneath the text – most important for a conductor of opera. Only then in his thorough and detailed way would *Maestro* work on the content of the recitatives and arias along with the language. He showed me how the sound comes alive not just through the Italian vowels but also through their being combined with the consonants. In this way I learned the inherent rhythm of Italian, and how it is translated into music. It was also eye-opening when he demonstrated that, unlike German opera where the strongest beat is usually the first in the bar, in Italian, in order to reproduce natural speech rhythms, the first note may come before or after the beat.

'For our Nikikai productions we had all the benefits of *Maestro*'s international experience. He was particularly sad about the lost opportunities for many Japanese singers who rely on recordings when learning their roles. As a result, they often don't pay attention to the meaning of the libretto and are unable to do justice to the emotion and drama of the opera. He tried to overcome this tendency by teaching the importance of understanding the text and building soloists' self-confidence in their individual voices and personalities.

'I am now based in Europe and, unfortunately, I don't have many opportunities to work with *Maestro* Gardini anymore. But I have had some interesting experiences, nonetheless, that keep him in my mind. Once Paolo Gavanelli – a famous baritone who has performed in Japan many times – was singing the title role in my production of *Macbeth* at La Monnaie. I made certain suggestions about phrasing which surprised him. He asked me where I got my ideas from. "Only Italian *maestri* from the time of Renata Tebaldi or Mario del Monaco know that interpretation. I cannot believe that a young Japanese like you would," he said. The same happened with Norma Fantini when we were doing some arias from *Aïda*. She had a special coach who is quite experienced and steeped in the Italian tradition. He was also intrigued. I told them that I'd been studying with a certain *Maestro* Gardini in Japan.

'Ubaldo Gardini is like a rich fountain of knowledge – the more we are ready to or wish to drink, the more water shall be pumped out.'

...as La Marquise de Berkenfield, *La Fille du Régiment*, The Royal Opera House Covent Garden

Felicity Palmer is one of today's most celebrated and versatile performing artists, equally at home in music as diverse as Wagner, Rossini, Dvorák, Beethoven, Handel and Berio. She performs regularly at the world's major opera venues, including the Metropolitan Opera House New York, the Royal Opera House Covent Garden, La Scala Milan and the Deutsche Oper Berlin, in roles such as Klytemnestra (*Elektra*), The Old Prioress (*Les Dialogues des Carmélites*), Mistress Quickly (*Falstaff*) and The Countess (*Pique Dame*).

Miss Palmer has long distinguished herself in concert performances with international orchestras under such acclaimed conductors as Boulez, Davis, Rozhdestvensky, Mackerras, Sinopoli, Harnoncourt and Rattle. She has also given recitals in London and throughout Europe. Her many recordings include Stravinsky's *Le Rossignol*, vocal music by Benjamin Britten, and Messiaen's *Poèmes pour Mi* with Pierre Boulez.

In addition to working privately with young professional singers in London, Miss Palmer also gives masterclasses in Europe and the USA. She was appointed a CBE in 1993.

Felicity Palmer worked on the following recordings with Ubaldo Gardini: La Cenerentola *and* Le Nozze di Figaro (*Sir Neville Marriner) along with* Lo sposo deluso (*Sir Colin Davis*).

'I think that good coaches are just as necessary nowadays – and that many young singers would be knocked senseless if they encountered Ubaldo. One was confronted with somebody who was a *maestro*, who seemed to know absolutely everything. He drove and drove until he got as much as he could out of people, and I responded to that. At first I often felt inadequate because I realised how little I knew and how much there was to do. Yet he never made you feel stupid. His passion for the Italian language came across so strongly that you had to go with it.

'I don't know where he got the energy from or how he sustained it but it was intoxicating. He also had the rare power of forcing you to go away and think about what you'd done. He knew that Italians would sniff us out especially when we were doing recordings where there had to be a unity of style. We had to sound as though we were Italian and to achieve that, of course, Ubaldo had to go over the top occasionally.

'He seemed to be on a crusade to transform British singers into Italians and he had to do it virtually overnight. I know how much energy it takes; he had to give 200 per cent all the time in order to get eighty back. It was as though his life depended on it. The adrenalin helps you do the work, but by the end of it, you're sapped beyond reason until nothing is left.

'I think some of Ubaldo has rubbed off on me. I feel passionate – also like somebody on a mission – about binding the text to the music and I work very slowly. Now here I am years later sitting with students, and I am the one working in this fastidious way because it interests me enormously.'

RUGGERO RAIMONDI

BASS-BARITONE

…in the title role, *Don Giovanni* the film, directed by Joseph Losey

One of the greatest lyric singers of our age, **Ruggero Raimondi** combines exceptional vocal qualities with an expressive stage presence, playing the major parts in the bass repertoire. He has performed at the world's most prestigious opera houses with the greatest conductors and directors. His favourite roles are: Don Giovanni, Philip II, Boris Godunov, Don Quixote and Thomas à Beckett.

Born in Bologna, Mr Raimondi's professional career was launched at the age of just 23 when he won the Spoleto prize for his performance of Colline in *La Bohème*. Contracts with Rome and other prominent Italian opera venues swiftly followed. In 1970, performances at the Metropolitan Opera House New York, the Royal Opera House Covent Garden and the Bayerische Staatsoper Munich established his international reputation.

Ruggero Raimondi has made many recordings with conductors such as Bernstein, Von Karajan, Giulini, Muti, Levine, Maazel and Abbado. He also has an accomplished film career, playing Don Giovanni in Joseph Losey's film of the same name, Escamillo in Francesco Rosi's *Carmen*, and Boris in Zulawski's *Boris Godunov*. His Scarpia in the television production of *Tosca*, (with Plácido Domingo and Catherine Malfitano), conducted by Zubin Mehta, was filmed in the exact locations where the opera's action takes place, and was seen live in 106 countries.

His recent roles include Iago, Falstaff and Don Alfonso. He has also successfully directed productions of *Don Giovanni, Il barbiere di Siviglia* and *Don Carlos*.

Ubaldo Gardini prepared Ruggero Raimondi for his roles as Don Giovanni both at Glyndebourne and the Royal Opera House Covent Garden. They also worked on several Philips recordings including La Cenerentola (*conducted by Sir Neville Marriner*); I Lombardi alla prima crociata, Attila *and* I masnadieri (*all conducted by Lamberto Gardelli*).

'I always thought Ubaldo was like a person coming from another world. When I did something completely new, he would scream with delight that finally we had found another way to express the feelings of the different characters on stage. We were Italian. We were free spirits who didn't want to be put inside a box or to be the kind of musicians for whom a performance is like a ticket to the theatre, that is to say, go, sing and come back. We wanted to create art and not just give routine, mechanical performances.

'When it comes to knowledge about the traditions of opera Ubaldo is a kind of encyclopedia. If you listen to what he says about the libretto, the music or conducting, you can learn a lot. I never thought about whether he had academic degrees or not because what he was telling me was so informative.

'Ubaldo was a searcher, and for English people, who are quite conservative, it may be difficult to understand that every time you produce something you must try to find a new approach. Sometimes the effort to innovate makes you try crazy things. So with some English singers it was difficult to explore different ideas because they were young, straight from music college, and learning roles for the first time.

'He and I had many discussions about *Don Giovanni* and its eponymous anti-hero. We built up the character slowly and carefully, after a lot of analysis. My belief now is that Don Giovanni works best if the performer is preferably young, has a lot of strength, personality, voice and a great dynamic range. But the sustaining element comes from the music of Mozart, especially in the recitatives. I don't sing Don Giovanni any more because I've done the role so many times.

'My basic philosophy is as follows: music has a regular rhythm, 1-2-3-4 in a bar. But let's try 1-2-2½-3-4. Let's give it life. We can be prepared, we can be professional, we can be perfectly in time, but let's be creative artists, not singing machines. That means we take risks, maybe even make a mistake, but so what? A good conductor can respond to that moment.

'I think Ubaldo had the same idea. He would laugh when I changed something while other singers remained fixed in their interpretations. And I would warn him when I wanted to try something new. He would often discourage me because I "could make trouble". But I would do it anyhow and the result was performances with spark, tension and interest.

'When I was young, all conductors were also great teachers of opera. Gradually, however, they have started coming from an orchestral background. They often think opera is easy. In fact, it is more difficult than symphonic music because the voice is not like an orchestral instrument, and the personality of the singer, while not exactly unstable, is always anxious, nervous. Ubaldo was someone who could get his singers to avoid this kind of fear. He would tell us, "Don't be afraid, the voice is there."'

AKEMI SAKAMOTO
MEZZO-SOPRANO

Regarded as one of Japan's leading soloists of international repute, prizewinning mezzo-soprano, **Akemi Sakamoto,** completed her studies to postgraduate level at Tokyo Geidai University of the Arts, subsequently winning a scholarship from the Italian government to study in Milan. With regular performances in both countries, she continues to divide her time between Italy and Japan.

Miss Sakamoto's roles have included Dorabella (*Così fan tutte*), Fenena (*Nabucco*), Rosina (*Il barbiere di Siviglia*) and the title role in *Carmen*, along with the Japanese characters, Chikara Oishi (*Chushingura*) and Princess Yamato (*Takeru*). Recent performances include Lola (*Cavalleria rusticana*), Bersi (*Andrea Chénier*) and Preziosilla (*La forza del destino*), all at the New National Theatre of Japan, Tokyo. She also played Azucena (*Il Trovatore*) as part of the Verdi Project at the Sainokuni Hall.

Akemi Sakamoto's concert repertoire has included Prokofiev's *Alexander Nevsky* (with the St Petersburg Philharmonic) and Beethoven's Symphony No 9 (with the Czech Philharmonic). In Japan, she has performed in Janácek's *Fate* and *Glagolithic Mass* with the Yomiiuri Symphony Orchestra, Wagner's *Wesendonck Lieder* with the Yamagata Symphony Orchestra, and Schoenberg's *Gurrelieder* with the Kyoto Symphony and the Tokyo Symphony orchestras.

Akemi Sakamoto has worked with Ubaldo Gardini on the following roles: Vitellia (La clemenza di Tito), *Azucena* (Il Trovatore) and *Suzuki* (Madama Butterfly).

'When I was in my final year of the MA course at Tokyo Geidai our opera production was Mozart's *La clemenza di Tito*. I had my first one-to-one recitative lesson with *Maestro* Gardini for the role of Vitellia. Over several years – including those when I was an undergraduate – I had been working my way through the *Arie antiche* [standard Italian vocal exercises] in the mistaken belief that my pronunciation was correct. I thought Italian was similar to Japanese and was shocked at how bad mine was, especially when I remembered how I had previously sung Cherubino without any worries. I was pronouncing what I saw on the page literally, without knowing the linguistic rules, nor the vocal physiology involved.

'Gardini-*sensei* patiently taught us how to produce the Italian sounds – for example, what has to happen in the mouth in order to form individual vowels and consonants – and then how to combine them. He also showed us how to move smoothly from one note to another. He explained how each individual word has to be beautiful and when joined together, the musical line should be as lovely and unbroken as a string of pearls. In this way I realised the importance of the libretto in Italian opera.

'With my patchy understanding of the text, I also became aware of the difficulty of conveying real emotion in my singing. We Japanese students had been so obsessed with trying to imitate the Italian style that we gave little thought to the meaning of the text. But *Maestro* Gardini wouldn't let one word go by without ensuring we fully understood what we were singing – including the range of possible interpretations of just one adjective. He even had to tell us which phrases were questions, commands, or merely exclamations.

'With regard to the Italian language, we had other problems to overcome. Musical terms such as *lento, adagio, presto* are frequently translated into Japanese. The pace for *andante*, irrespective of the piece of music and its context, is often decided by the gauge on one of our "superb" Japanese metronomes. For *accelerando* we just sang faster, regardless of the libretto or our individual physiques.

'I have never met a teacher as strict as *Maestro* Gardini. He was a stickler for detail. Endless corrections and his final declaration, "OK, not too bad", usually signifies that my pronunciation is correct and I am expressing as best I can the essence of the words. There are other coaches whose approach to singing is more technical, but Gardini-*sensei*'s greatness lies in his ability to make the non-Italian singer express all the beauty of the libretto and the music in a true Italian way.

'His approach makes my body feel free from stress and my voice natural and comfortable. I've read many technical books about singing – from breathing technique to posture – but I find that thanks to my lessons with *Maestro*, I've incorporated those elements into my performance quite unconsciously.

'I can easily apply his principles to other languages – such as Latin, French and Spanish. When I work with different pianists or conductors, they don't have many problems with me. This has given me a confidence I wouldn't otherwise have.

'Not everybody has the same concepts as Gardini-*sensei* and nowadays, of course, I often have to compromise in order to do what a director wants, even though it might be different from what I've learned. But I make this conscious choice from a position of knowledge. Anyway, I've also come to realise that in singing, as in other aspects of music, we are all aiming at the same musical objective, despite our different approaches.'

A PERSONAL VIEW OF ROSSINI

A PERSONAL VIEW OF ROSSINI

Ubaldo Gardini

[An edited article previously published in *Opera Guides No 36, in association with English National Opera and The Royal Opera*. Series Editor: Nicholas John.]

Maestro Gardini has coached singers and advised on performances at The Royal Opera House, Covent Garden, the Metropolitan Opera House, New York, the Juilliard School and the Tokyo [Geidai] *University of the Arts. This is an edited transcript of a tape-recording he made in answer to various points put to him by the Editor.*

Today singers perform every type of vocal music, most of the time forced to compete with the overwhelming sonority of the modern orchestra. How can they possibly do justice to the variety of styles which have arisen in the evolution of vocal art? In Rossini's time there were very celebrated established schools of singing. Their motto was: 'One is born a singer, but one becomes an artist by studying for the whole of one's life'. 'Cantare' meant singing *dolce, piano, expressive, con sentimento*. Early 19th-century Italian opera was for the great heart of the people, not just for intellectuals.

Rossini and his colleagues knew the natural resources of the human voice. They were themselves singers, and their orchestras never dominated the dramatic action. Rapid and clear scenes infused with simple but human emotions were congenial to the Italian temperament. The orchestra was light, aiming in its own way at enabling singers to sing expressively and very rhythmically – one might say 'dancing'; not as square-cut and over-accentuated as today. The word was always of cardinal importance ('la parola musicata'), and this involved a concentration on the emotive expression of the singing voice and its marriage to the orchestral sound.

In a letter to Arrivabene, Verdi wrote: 'In *The Barber*, the phrase "Signor, giudizio, per carità" is neither melody nor harmony; it is the declaimed word, just true and essentially music.' In practically every phrase of *The Barber* we can see it was 'la parola' that gave birth spontaneously to the music. To take just one example, it is evidently the verbal line 'Pace e gioia sia con voi' which inspired the musical line, such is the naturalness of the Italian verbal expression, and the way it is accentuated in the music. It can also be seen in the dynamic variety of the recitatives. Rossini wrote as an Italian speaks, thinks and feels, full of warmth and enthusiasm, of joy and sorrow; he knew how to use the national idiom, and composed what Byron called 'musica favellata' or – which is difficult to translate – 'spoken music', where the same delivery is given to musical phrases as to spoken words. Stendhal wrote: 'The Rossinian revolution has killed the originality of the singers. They are condemned to find everything already prepared for them.' So it seems that even Rossini may be given the accolade for a reform, or even a revolution! His enemies, and the mere virtuosi fanciers, said that 'with him the bel canto ceased to exist'. And later they were to say the same to Verdi – he was also supposed to ruin voices.

Monaldi has described a performance in Milan of Rossini's *Aureliano in Palmira* when the celebrated Velluti started to ornament his part with inimitable agility. Rossini, he said, did not find all this *fioritura* to his taste, but done in that impeccable way it produced an admirable effect. Yet in 1813 Rossini wrote to Cicognara, 'the sense of time, that essential part of the music, without which neither melody nor harmony can be understood... is violated and ignored by singers. Their aim is to surprise instead of to move; and where, in the old days, the aim of the instrumental players was to sing like singers, with their instruments, now the singers studied to play with their voices like instrumentalists.' Knowing all the abuses of egocentric singers like La Marcolini, La Marchesi and La Colbran, Rossini thought he would embellish his melodies himself according to their particular abilities so as to prepare a uniform style for them and, in so doing, to ensure a unity in their performances.

Thus, he was really responsible for restoring the melodic line to his scores – still in an adorned form, but capable of sincerity and meaning in performance. At the same time one cannot deny that the virtuosi of that period had an incomparable vocal dexterity, and superlative control of every aspect of the human voice. As a result, any voice (whether soprano, contralto, tenor or bass) could tackle extremely difficult passages and sustain the same tessitura. Voices trained in that one, and only one, way (and in the way best suited to them, so as to exhibit what they considered their best features) could, for instance, equally well sing as what today we call a soprano (whether lyric or leggiero) or as a contralto.

Looking through Rossini's many operas, one cannot but be astonished at the extraordinary variety and versatility of his creative imagination. But one thing stands out as the cornerstone of his temperament: the comic. The *opera buffa* belongs to the Italians, to the joy of their contagious laughter. And Rossini communicates this particular joy in that particular style of his time, more free and intense than that, for example, of Cimarosa, which is more restrained, more innocent, more tender and gracious. Rossini already belongs to a more modern time. He does not depict Beaumarchais's Figaro, but a typically Italian ambience full of Roman intrigue and self-interested people whose lives bubble with comedy – and caustic irony too!

Let us now examine the requirements for performance of Rossini's music. He wrote for voices with a considerable range and asked for exceptional flexibility rather than a mere display of virtuosity – for an expressive coloratura. This really means he wanted colours with which the voice could paint each note, independent of their velocity or intensity, treating each note as a *messa di voce*, like a 'pearl'. Never sing roughly; sing elegantly and aesthetically.

Regarding style: it is one of the hardest things an artist can achieve, much more difficult than more advanced or complex compositions. It is based on the *commedia dell'arte* and requires the singer to be able to act with his voice and his whole body, with a voice both natural and free, and to avoid like the plague 'phoney' opera acting and singing. In Rossini's time all the straight actors of the *teatro di prosa* were encouraged to see and hear singers on the operatic stage. Much has been written about this; the best-known text is by the Italian poet Gian Giulio Barrilli, but there is also the less-known, though extraordinary, book by Franceschini, *L'arte della parola*, 'On the art of the word'. He recommends that actors listen to the sublime interpretations of singers in Rossini's operas specifically in order to learn how to act and how to declaim effectively. The primary interest does not lie in quavers and semiquavers, *Ars longa vita brevis*, and it cannot be measured with a conductor's baton.

Regarding Rossini traditions (and not only his): one must always be very cautious. Under such pretexts one is so often forced to tolerate the most absurd oddities. Some are logical, and one can see why they have survived, but most of the time they are illegal. And so are 'cuts' – not that one always wants to do a work in its entirety, especially in Italian opera; just because cuts have always been made in a certain way, however, is not a sufficient reason for us to accept them. Italian opera must always be treated with a sense of interpretative freedom; by reading between the notes, music can be given life and spontaneity. A never-ending aim is to make it live, really live. Leonardo said 'simplicity is so difficult to achieve', and in that single statement one can sum up Italian opera in general. Its elements are just what are essentially necessary and sufficient, and in this apparent simplicity lie the great difficulties; success or failure rests on the shoulders of the artists alone. Italian music especially needs an interpreter, a true interpreter. This idea of 'freedom' to which I referred above, must not be misunderstood; the *tempo rubato* in the hands of someone who, however intellectually prepared, does not have an impeccable rhythmic sense is disastrous.

About the words: opera was born out of poetry. The poets were singers. We know from Caccini: 'Prima le parole, poi il ritmo, poi le note; e non per il contrario.' ('First the words, then the rhythm, then the notes, and not the other way around.) The words have always been of supreme importance for every Italian artist, even painters, architects, sculptors. Apart from the fact that the Italian language has been universally recognised as the most beautiful for singing, and that 'parlate bene e cantate bene' ('speak beautifully and you will sing beautifully'), or 'si parla come si canta, o si canta come si parla' ('one speaks as one sings, and one sings as one speaks'), for us music without the voice, without the metaphysical power of the voice, never meant much at all. So pronunciation from that part of Italy where opera was born is the prime requisite for a modern singer. Italians, too, not born in Tuscany, must learn, like any foreigner, that beauty of utterance. Manzoni, for example, studied for a long time in Florence, and, at the end, said, 'a peasant in Tuscany is a much greater poet than myself'.

Furthermore, Italian poetry is very allusive, very ambiguous, with many second meanings, metaphors and allegories, which can only be understood if the lines are well rendered. Italian poetry is written to be read aloud. Italians call this art of speaking poetry, rhetoric; the emphasis on elocution, and the overstressed approach that one hears so persistently do not belong to our way of delivering poetry. Italian derives from Latin and it is a melodic, not a stressed, language. Generally, we aim to stress one important syllable, usually towards the end of a sentence, and so towards the end of a musical phrase. To perform Rossini, as for all Italian composers, you must be a master of speaking correctly: 'l'arte del dire' is everything. The pauses, also, must be full of interest and pulsating rhythm, and not merely stopping and resting places as we call pauses in English. Verdi said: 'Vivere le pause' (Long live the pause!) – do not treat them as rests, but bridge them. If you take a rest, the public goes to sleep.

To sing with that beautiful and correct pronunciation is easy compared to rendering *recitativo secco* or *strumentato*. Here, the real artists truly emerge; the actor-singer here can excel, because everything depends on him alone. The drama, the colour, the speed, the pauses; music here is only a blueprint, schematically, conventionally written, and depends on the artist to make it alive and true. Everything which happens in the drama is said in the recitatives. So they are more difficult to perform than a concerto and must be studied as carefully! And when recitatives are followed by arias and ensembles etc., they must be integrated and joined in a logical, rhythmical way that gives no sense of close to the ending of the recitative, but of continuity and inexorability to the unfolding of the lyric drama, which must be an entity from beginning to end.

We must finally turn to the Italians' much criticised habit of repeating themselves, especially in opera. When an Italian speaks, he generally repeats himself, and he elaborates and divagates; so in opera. Yes, it is one of our national characteristics. As soon as an Italian says something, he immediately thinks he has expressed it badly; in a word, that he has given a bad performance. And so he tries to do better by repeating it, until he has satisfied himself or, especially, he has his listener's approving consent. So please, whenever you have to repeat a phrase in Rossini's operas, aim always to improve the way you sing it; and, of course, you must always try to improve at every later performance. The saying 'Paganini non ripete', ('Paganini does not repeat'), applies to all of us. You cannot expect Italian artists to be constant. Every night they try to do better, and they are different in every way, to the dismay of the conductors, directors – of everyone who is not Italian. So in this case we use the English saying 'Variety is the spice of life'.

[Reprinted with kind permission from Calder Publications Ltd.]

MEET THE ARTISTS

Biographies & Interviews Part Four

...in the title role, *Madama Butterfly*, Vienna State Opera House

One of Japan's best-known singers in concert and opera, **Shinobu Sato** made her Japanese debut as Violetta in *La Traviata*. She has subsequently given acclaimed performances in such roles as Tosca and Madama Butterfly – the latter reprised for her debut at the Vienna State Opera House in 1998, and more recently at the Victoria State Opera House Melbourne.

Miss Sato has sung with leading international orchestras under conductors including Sir Colin Davis, Charles Dutoit, Christoph Eschenbach, Eliahu Inbal, Seiji Ozawa and Christian Thielemann. In her native Japan, she has won many prestigious awards, such as the Giraud Grand Opera Prize, the Japan Cultural Broadcasting Music Award and the Metropolitan Cultural Honour.

Her recordings of opera arias made in Europe include Mozart with Hans-Martin Schneidt conducting the Berlin Radio Symphony Orchestra, and others of Verdi and Puccini.

Shinobu Sato's work with Ubaldo Gardini for the Nasa Opera Company Japan includes Le Nozze di Figaro, La serva padrona *and* Tosca.

'When I first worked with *Maestro* Gardini in 1992 as the Countess in *Le Nozze di Figaro*, it was an eye-opening encounter with an authentic Italian *bel canto* coach. With all the arias and recitatives, it was a very demanding role, but I found myself looking forward to rehearsals as never before.

'At the beginning there were some difficulties of communication and I often had no idea what *Maestro* was trying to teach us. One typical example concerns the *fermata*. I remember him once shouting, "Pulse, pulse", at a pause in my line and telling me to place my fingers on my wrist. At first I couldn't see why I should be measuring my pulse when I'd stopped singing. But what he was trying to demonstrate was the important rule of Western music: that even during the *fermata* the pulse must be maintained.

'I recall something else from those early days. Once we were very solemnly (and beautifully!) singing some passage in a Mozart with a typical Da Ponte libretto and noticed him in fits of laughter. When we finished he explained a risqué double meaning that had gone right over our heads.

'To be an Italian coach, it is not enough to point out basic errors in our singing. The score is very important, too, and *Maestro* has many different editions. After a lifetime of scrutiny and comparing, he can readily spot mistakes in the one I might be using. However, we Japanese have no alternative but to work from the most popular version. As a result, our interpretations can be rather stereotyped or inaccurate. For instance, a printing error can put a breath mark in a line which should be sung without a break. But by ourselves we wouldn't know it's wrong.

'While he is passionate about music and art, it is *Maestro* Gardini's warmth and rapport with his singers that has most impressed me. This is what enables him to persist with his strict way of teaching. I appreciate the opportunity to work with someone who reciprocates our affection and shows his belief in us even though we are so inexperienced.'

FREDERICA VON STADE

MEZZO-SOPRANO

…as Elena, *La donna del lago*, The Royal Opera House Covent Garden

Described by the *New York Times* as one of America's finest artists, **Frederica von Stade** made her debut at the Metropolitan Opera House New York in 1970 – the 30th anniversary of which was celebrated there with a specially-staged, new production of *The Merry Widow*. Her international repertoire includes roles in operas by Mozart, Massenet, Debussy, Berlioz, Strauss and Rossini. Miss von Stade has appeared with every major American opera company, and has also had new productions mounted for her in Europe at La Scala Milan, the Royal Opera House Covent Garden, the Vienna State Opera and the Paris Opéra.

Miss von Stade has also performed at the world's leading concert and recital halls. Her recordings (many prize-winning) include complete operas, aria collections, symphonic works, solo recitals and crossover albums. She appears regularly on television in the USA through PBS and other networks. The holder of awards and honours there and in Europe, her engagements as both opera singer and concert artist continue unabated.

At the start of her career, Frederica von Stade worked with Ubaldo Gardini on the following roles, mainly at Glyndebourne: Cherubino (Le Nozze di Figaro), *Sesto* (La clemenza di Tito), *the title role* (La Cenerentola) *and Penelope* (Il ritorno d'Ulisse in patria).

'Glyndebourne was magical. You worked twelve satisfying hours a day, interspersed with plenty of rewarding breaks. I learned a lot from my training there with Ubaldo – for instance, how good singing is the result of dedication and discipline. Scotto – and Callas who spent each summer working on her great voice with De Sabata – exemplify this very well.

'Ubaldo also took the mystery out of *bel canto*, and showed us that it's not just a pretty tune floating above a lovely accompaniment. Nor is it a talent or accident. Rather, it's a very specific study. To sing a great composer like Bellini, you need all your vocal skills, such as how to do the *messa di voce* [placing of the voice to sustain long notes], sing a trill, do beautiful *crescendos, decrescendos, portamen-*

tos – all these along with keeping the vowels pure and at the same time conveying the different emotions the character is feeling.

'I remember Ubaldo's great devotion to the language of the libretto. He taught us how to show off the Italian words in the most beautiful way so that the meaning is clear. Maybe if I'd been born in Italy or started aged ten it would have been easier. But I sure loved trying for it, because all of a sudden I could sing those pure vowels and double consonants – or words like "*pianto*" as three syllables – exactly as written and not in our American way as two, with a "*y*" like "*pya-nto*".

'I rarely sing a phrase without thinking of Ubaldo. He is the kind of inspirational coach who takes the music apart and then puts it back together again, so that you understand exactly what you're doing. No linguistic or musical detail is too small. If there's a word on a triplet, he insists the stresses be placed on exactly the right notes.

'You needed incredible stamina to keep up with him in those days. His energy, enthusiasm and athleticism filled the room and by the end of a coaching session you needed a Valium!

'On the other hand, Ubaldo also has a very spiritual side to his personality and is a devout Catholic who often seemed to see music in terms of symbols. His scores were full of mysterious, multi-coloured markings. To us young singers back then they seemed like a secret code. There were also lots of triangles – which can denote the idea of the Trinity in Roman Catholic theology. Maybe to him they represented sublime moments in Puccini or Verdi that took you up to God.'

ROBIN STAPLETON
CONDUCTOR

Robin Stapleton trained at London's Royal College of Music and subsequently at the London Opera Centre, where he was the Royal Opera House Covent Garden scholar. He then joined the Opera House music staff – at the time the youngest-ever *répétiteur* and chorus director in the theatre's history.

His work there included productions of *Tosca, La Bohème, Madama Butterfly, Macbeth, Der Freischütz* and *Die Fledermaus,* with singers including Bergonzi, Domingo, Pavarotti, Ricciarelli, Caballé, Freni and Te Kanawa.

Robin Stapleton opened the new Johannesburg opera house in South Africa, conducting *La Traviata* with Alfredo Kraus and Giorgio Zancanaro. Other international engagements have included *Carmen* (Mexico City), *La Traviata* (Netherlands Opera), *Falstaff* (Gothenberg), *Tosca* (Royal Opera House Japan tour) and *La Bohème* (Opera San Diego).

Formerly a frequent performer on BBC television and radio, Robin Stapleton now gives masterclasses in association with Dame Kiri Te Kanawa, as well as continuing to appear on UK and European concert platforms. His CD with the Royal Liverpool Philharmonic Orchestra was released in October 2006.

Robin Stapleton worked with Ubaldo Gardini, both as a répétiteur *and later as a conductor, on operas including* Don Giovanni, Le Nozze di Figaro, Così fan tutte *and* La Bohème.

'I first met Ubaldo in 1967 when I was still a student at the London Opera Centre where he was doing some teaching. The following year I had the good fortune to join the music staff at the Royal Opera House where he had just become Italian coach. We went through "thick and thin" together until 1979.

'I eventually became Chorus Master and, thanks to Colin Davis, began conducting in the mid-1970s. By this time Ubaldo had become essential to the preparation of the Italian repertoire, not only for his knowledge of the language but also his understanding of the *bel canto* style and how to use words so that the music emerged to convey a complete concept. It is difficult to explain, but the Italian language to Ubaldo was a musical instrument that you played, and the result was tone of the same quality as a Stradivarius in the hands of a great virtuoso. He had a major influence on me especially regarding orchestral string colour and, in particular, bowing and fingering. Musicians sometimes became irritated when he seemed to interfere with these technical elements. But most of them did recognise his obvious gifts concerning both vocal and instrumental sound.

'Some *répétiteurs* resented playing for Ubaldo's coaching sessions. They thought it a waste of their time. I didn't. Working on a Mozart recitative with him was always a revelation, and now when I am preparing singers I feel I should send my fees to Ubaldo knowing that I am just repeating what he taught me. His analysis of text was both fascinating and entertaining, especially regarding *double entendres*. For example, his explanation of Musetta's waltz song (*La Bohème*) is quite unprintable and, to some students, unrepeatable!

'Ubaldo gave me important advice on conducting: "Always remember the upbeat is life and the downbeat is death. So never accent it when it is not called for." He also possessed a natural sense of timing and pace, as essential to a conductor as to an actor or comedian. When we got them wrong he would hold his head in his hands and yell, "No. *Aspetta*!" [Wait!]

'I honestly think that I have Ubaldo to thank for ninety percent of what I have learned about Italian opera, and a great amount about music in general. On the other hand, his punctuality was often erratic, to say the least. He never knew when to stop working – nor often when to start! There were times when he didn't appear at all. On tour in Japan he went missing for three days, but that's another story.'

...as Colline, *La Bohème*, Tokyo Bunka Kaikan

Keizo Takahashi is currently professor of Italian Opera at Tokyo Music College. He was Executive Director of their 2007 centenary production of *Le Nozze di Figaro*, and performed the title role. Originally from Fukushima Prefecture in northern Japan, he is a graduate of Tokyo Geidai University of the Arts.

A winner of several prizes including the Japan Music Concours and the Giro Opera Competition, Mr Takahashi is a member of several Japanese opera companies including the Tokyo Nikikai, Fujiwara and the New National Theatre. Especially acclaimed for his König Heinrich in *Lohengrin*, his wide-ranging roles include Sarastro (*Die Zauberflöte*), Don Alfonso (*Così fan tutte*), Dr Dulcamara (*L'elisir d'amore*), Herman (*Tannhäuser*), Fiesco (*Simon Boccanegra*), Scarpia (*Tosca*) and, most recently, Figaro (*Le Nozze di Figaro*). He also enjoys a successful concert career having performed with the NHK (Japanese Broadcasting Corporation) Symphony Orchestra under Sawallisch, Maazel and Blomstedt.

Keizo Takahashi was coached by Ubaldo Gardini for the following roles: Dr Dulcamara (L'elisir d'amore), *Figaro* (Le Nozze di Figaro), *and others for productions at Tokyo Geidai, Tokyo Nikikai and Tokyo Music College.*

'I first met *Maestro* Gardini during Tokyo Geidai's production of *Le Nozze di Figaro* in 1985. That was the year I started teaching singing – and performing baritone roles – in the opera department there. In 1986, I sang Dulcamara in *L'elisir d'amore* under his direction.

'This opera is very difficult and without *Maestro* Gardini's work on the phrasing, breathing, pronunciation and other elements, I couldn't have succeeded in the role. Dulcamara's lines are particularly challenging – very wordy and typical *opera buffa* – for example, the rapid singing of names of medicines and illnesses. Nonetheless, I feel that this was one of my best-ever performances. I often ask myself, how could *Maestro* Gardini produce such a miracle? He's a perfectionist who believes in you and never gives up until he's pushed you to your limits and you make progress. Training with him is a totally absorbing experience. The preparation is technical – counting syllables, keeping the pulse, singing the libretto as though there are no bar lines, and so on. Recitatives are particularly difficult. Doing them the Japanese way, that is, with too much lip and mouth movement, causes all sorts of problems that he then has to correct.

'*Maestro* Gardini's way of working is particularly good for eliminating some other faults. For instance, many singers tend to equate opera singing with big voices, so they develop an artificial sound – all without any real understanding of the libretto. To curb these tendencies, *Maestro* ensures that you fully understand what you're singing and that you respond personally to the language, employing your own unique vocal colour.

'Gardini's productions are full of love and life. There are two points on which he will never compromise. He won't let anyone go against what is written in the score, nor will he tolerate cold, lifeless music-making where the singer is not fully engaged. These situations make him unhappy and angry.

'It was good to have a chance to prepare an opera with him where everybody could benefit from his experience and approach. This was the 2002 *Don Giovanni* for Tokyo Music College which was such a great success. Since I was producing and not performing, it was the first time I could observe his realistic staging and how the music, singing and acting came together so well. It was like watching a film. I don't know of anyone else who exemplifies as he does the integrated art that is opera.'

...coaching a scene from *Tosca* at the Fazioli Studio, Jaques Samuel Pianos, London, 2008 (with background mural of Canaletto's Venice)

Phillip Thomas was born in Neath, South Wales, and studied at the Royal Academy of Music in London, where he was a Countess of Munster scholar. As a student, he worked as *répétiteur* for Welsh National Opera. Upon graduation he was invited to join the staff of English National Opera where he is currently Casting Associate and also Head of Training for the Young Singers' Programme. He also enjoys a prolific concert career with performances throughout the UK, Ireland and the USA, as well as in Sydney, Tokyo, Buenos Aires and Taipei. He is the official accompanist for the BBC Cardiff Singer of the World competition.

Phillip Thomas has worked with such artists as Dame Josephine Barstow, Susan Bullock, Jane Eaglen, Dame Anne Evans, Lesley Garrett, Sergei Leiferkus, Felicity Palmer, Joan Rodgers, Nicola Rossi-Giordano, Sir John Tomlinson and Alan Woodrow. He has also worked as Vocal Consultant on productions and recordings for the BBC, BMG, Chandos, Decca, EMI and Sony. Currently, he is developing his career in conducting with performances including Verdi's *La Traviata, Rigoletto* and *Ernani* for the English National Opera and gala concerts with the distinguished tenor, Dennis O'Neill.

Phillip Thomas worked with Ubaldo Gardini on many operas including Tosca, Aïda *and* I pagliacci (*mainly at the English National Opera*). *He also accompanied many artists being prepared by Ubaldo for their roles elsewhere and for recordings.*

'I joined the English National Opera after graduating from the Royal Academy of Music and was lucky to form a very close musical relationship with the conductor, Mark Elder. He had learned his style of operatic coaching from Ubaldo, and I in turn, studied how to be a vocal coach from him. So when I met Ubaldo himself a few years later – in 1979 or 1980 when he came to do *Aïda* at the Coliseum – I felt I was at last in the presence of the great *maestro*. In those days, there was much more time to prepare a production, in contrast to today when singers are expected to be ready to perform after as little as two coaching sessions. It's fast-track opera, like fast food.

'People often say to me when I play for rehearsals that I sound like an orchestra, and wonder how I do it. The truth is, every time I accompany an aria, I feel I have the sword of Damocles above my head. But instead, it's Gardini. I remember once spending twenty minutes on one phrase of Verdi's *Rigoletto*. Finally, I said, "Ubaldo, this is impossible to do on the piano." He insisted it wasn't. He took the phrase apart, showed me what he wanted and how it should be played. Then we put it back together again. He was right and I did it – not once, but forever afterwards.

'Ubaldo never discussed technique. He would talk about the language, about not chewing words nor opening the mouth too wide. His favourite line in persuasion was to say to a singer, "if you open your mouth like this, you'll get lockjaw. You're too attractive".

'When we did the Verdi Requiem, the aria "Mors stupebit" was a revelation. Somebody was singing "mors" as though it were one syllable. "No, no, no," Ubaldo cried, "there are four sounds, *m–o–r–s*!" What a word it then becomes. To render it monosyllabically is an aberration. The singer doesn't use any more voice and the audience won't know what's being done technically. But they will hear the commanding delivery and that it sounds right.

'Ubaldo also gave you the courage to understand and analyse what's on the page and to do what you believe it says – not regurgitate what you might hear in a recording. I'll never forget him saying, "Phillip, ignore tradition. Tradition is always somebody's memory of the last bad performance they heard." I found that so liberating – he gave me the confidence to develop my own ideas.'

ALAN TITUS

BASS-BARITONE

...as Wotan, *Die Walküre*, Bayreuth Festival

New York-born **Alan Titus** studied at the renowned Juilliard School of Music and made his debut at the Washington Opera, playing Marcello in *La Bohème*. Major roles in the Italian, French and German repertoire followed, with appearances at all the leading opera houses in the USA, under conductors including Pritchard, Levine, Bonynge, Maazel and Bernstein.

Over the past decade, Alan Titus has concentrated on his career in Europe. After his Amsterdam debut he became a regular guest at the Bayerische Staatsoper Munich, enjoying success in a variety of roles under the baton of Wolfgang Sawallisch. These were quickly followed by engagements in Europe's other prominent opera venues with such conductors as Celebidache, Dorati, Kubelík, Maazel, Haitink, Thielemann, Dohnányi and Sinopoli.

Mr Titus made a successful transition to *Heldenbaritone* roles with performances of Barak (*Die Frau ohne Schatten*) and Hans Sachs (*Die Meistersinger von Nürnberg*) in 1992 and 1993 respectively. His roles – several prize-winning – have since included Wotan and the Wanderer at the Bayreuth Festival, as well as Kurwenal, the Flying Dutchman, Iago, Macbeth, Scarpia and Falstaff.

Alan Titus worked with Ubaldo Gardini on the title role of Don Giovanni (*at the Metropolitan Opera House New York, and later for a recording with Rafael Kubelík*), *and Count Almaviva* (Le Nozze di Figaro, *Glyndebourne*). *He was also coached privately by Ubaldo on the roles of Pagliacci and Guglielmo, and for a recording* of Le Nozze di Figaro (*Davis*). *He also worked with him in Japan and Germany.*

'It must have been in the early 1980s that I first met Ubaldo. We were both at the New York Metropolitan Opera House and I was preparing to make my debut in *Don Giovanni*. At the time I was with Columbia Artists, and Matthew Epstein, my manager, recommended Ubaldo because Frederica von Stade and Richard Stillwell had prepared roles with him. Ubaldo's kind of coaching, his violin experience, plus his years at Covent Garden, provided a level of preparation that was new to me. He had this extraordinary quality of finding meaning in operas that was not only cross-cultural but also – I don't know if there's a word for this – cross-century, with the 19th century's aesthetics and culture his speciality.

'Ubaldo's perception of music was of its belonging to the larger universe of the arts and humanities. So, I think the term "musician" is too restrictive. In fact, he saw himself more as a philosopher and poet. I remember once getting out of a taxi in Munich with him and the cab driver perceptively referring to him as *einer alter Kavalier* – an old knight.

'We often talked about poetry. I recall once sitting on the banks of the Isar in Munich and his showing me how several different poems by Petrarch had been set to music. He always said to look at the original poem because words – even meanings – can be changed in the setting or the printing. We then scrutinised several examples. I've never forgotten this lesson in musicology, so now I ensure that I work with the most authentic version of a score that I can find.

'Ubaldo had memorable ways of putting a point across. I remember studying *Figaro* with him where my first word as the Count is "Susanna". As I pronounced the "*s*" he must have stopped me about fifty times to try and show me the way it is pronounced in Italian. He explained that it is a very breathy, sexy sound and that Da Ponte obviously knew what he was doing when he started the Count's opening line with "*Sssssssuuzanna*".

'Ubaldo also said that in Italian the bar lines in the score are called *stanga*, something like metal bars. So when we were reading the music his advice was mentally to remove the bar lines so as to see the phrase as one stream of sound and to concentrate on the thought behind it. In Wagner, in Verdi and when you listen to old De Sabata and Giulini recordings, you hear that in action.

'The *Don Giovanni* in which I was involved – Rafael Kubelík's last recording – is basically all Ubaldo's work. I sang an aria for Kubelík and he took me right away because he could see I knew what I was doing. Ubaldo's coaching had ensured my arrival on the international stage.'

SUMIKO TOKUSHIMA
ACCOMPANIST & RÉPÉTITEUR

Born in Osaka, Japan, **Sumiko Tokushima** has been attached to the music staff of Tiroler Landestheater since 1994. She graduated from the Musashino Academy of Music near Tokyo, and began her professional career as *répétiteur* for the Japanese Opera Union. She then became rehearsal accompanist and *répétiteur* at Tokyo's Bunkamura Opera Theatre, where she worked under the *maestri* Kazushi Ono, Neil Varon and Renato Palumbo – for *Die Zauberflöte, L'elisir d'amore, Hänsel und Gretel, Samson et Dalila, La Bohème, Rigoletto, La Traviata* and *Madama Butterfly*. She was later engaged to work with Patrick Summers on the San Francisco Opera Center production of *La Bohème*.

Miss Tokushima enjoys a close association with many Japanese opera companies including Yokohama City Opera, Japan Opera Foundation and the Lirica Italiana Opera. Her versatile keyboard skills have also won her engagements with the Tokyo Philharmonic and Tokyo Symphony orchestras, playing piano, celeste, harmonium and harpsichord.

As a frequent concert accompanist and chamber musician, Miss Tokushima has participated in recordings for NHK (Japanese Broadcasting Corporation) and ORF (Austrian Broadcasting Corporation).

Sumiko Tokushima is one of Ubaldo Gardini's most frequent coaching-accompanists. Her engagements for him have included: Madama Butterfly (Tokyo Geidai / *San Francisco Opera Center joint production 1989*), *an Opera Aria Concert* (*Niigata Citizen's Opera*) *and numerous others.*

'I have been working with *Maestro* Gardini for about fifteen years now. I first met him when I was at university and went along to play for a friend who was having a singing lesson. When in 1989 Tokyo Geidai and San Francisco Opera Center had a joint workshop in Japan on *Madama Butterfly*, I was given the opportunity to have further tuition. Later, he invited me to be his accompanist when he did some work in Europe, for instance at the Bregenz Music Festival, the Salzburg Festival and Tiroler Landestheater Innsbruck.

'*Maestro* Gardini is an excellent teacher, who after a lifetime of study and experience offers original interpretation and insights into the Italian operatic repertory. He knows what he wants and expects his students to achieve it, especially by observing the smallest details. Nevertheless, when they encounter something difficult or make mistakes, he is never negative.

'Some elements that we studied all those years ago only begin to make sense now. This applies not just to accompanying but also to art and music in general. For example, only when I moved away from Japan did I realise the invaluable role of the piano, up to the point where the orchestra takes over, in rehearsing and preparing an opera.

'In contrast to Europe, it is not easy in Japan for a good pianist to make a living as an accompanist. Had I stayed in my own country, a career such as I enjoy in Innsbruck would have been impossible. Not only do I have to express myself confidently through my playing but I have to share what I think with instrumentalists, conductors and producers. For a Japanese like myself, brought up in a consensus culture, discouraged from having or expressing individual opinions, this is something that can be difficult to learn. But thanks to *Maestro* Gardini, I feel confident about my viewpoints and my interpretations of what I play – even to the extent of persuading other musicians with whom I work.'

...as Pancho Villa in *Concierto para Mendez*, Los Angeles Opera

After winning the Metropolitan Opera National Auditions in 1988, **LeRoy Villanueva** was awarded an Adler Fellowship with the San Francisco Opera Center. As a member of its Merola Opera Program, he received the Schwabacher Memorial First Prize, and sang in Western Opera Theater's 1988–9 tour which included performances in Japan, Guam, Saipan and China. He was the first recipient of the prestigious Lotos Foundation Award which resulted in his New York debut at the Carnegie Weill (Recital) Hall.

Mr Villanueva has sung in many leading opera houses in the USA, Canada and Europe, including Los Angeles, San Francisco, Houston, Montreal, Geneva and Dresden. In Paris, he has appeared in premieres including Phillipe Fenelon's *Salammbô* (as Spendius, Opéra National de Paris), and *Le Chevalier Imaginaire* (as Sancho Panza, Théâtre du Châtelet).

LeRoy Villanueva's concert career includes appearances with orchestras such as the Los Angeles Philharmonic, San Francisco Symphony, Chicago Symphony, Detroit Symphony, the Minnesota, Orchestre de la Suisse Romande and Tokyo Symphony. He has recorded the role of Ulisse in Monteverdi's *Il ritorno d'Ulisse in patria* and has appeared in a film of Menotti's *Amahl and the Night Visitors*, made by the BBC. Currently, Mr Villanueva is collaborating with the Los Angeles Opera Company writing new works for adults and young children.

LeRoy Villanueva worked with Ubaldo Gardini in Japan on the role of Sharpless in Madama Butterfly (*Tokyo Geidai / San Francisco Opera Center joint production*).

'I regarded Ubaldo more as a conductor than a coach. He was someone who, rather than just telling you to sing a certain way, brought all the elements together. With a vision of every aspect of the piece, he gave us a lot of new ideas about *Madama Butterfly*, such as the similarities between Japanese and Italian culture, Puccini's love of Japan – even the composer's interest in Buddhist philosophy.

'We were doing the Brescia version of the opera which is a much harsher statement against American imperialism than the well-known Paris edition. And it did change the way I interpreted my character, Sharpless. (Was he a part of the scheme in some way? Maybe, maybe not.) Ubaldo gave you insights into the role, and made the point that a careful reading of the libretto means that opera, like true drama, can be ambiguous. Every day we got some extra information about the history of the piece, such as the aria that isn't in the later Paris edition. Questions would be thrown at us. "Why did Puccini do this? What was the significance? And how did it change the opera?". We were always talking about these things. Ubaldo wasn't just "directing traffic".

'He showed how the musical interpretation is inseparable from the language and, conversely, how the language itself is part of the music. He would ask us to reflect on the context of the aria so as to give more colour. That approach can make a big difference to the way you sing a phrase, in respect of the tone quality and overall performance.

'Nor did musical minutiae escape his notice – he had such an attentive ear. He was someone who could say something that would actually end up changing your technique. You wanted to study with him because of what he knew about the voice and singing in Italian. There were things like the need to bring out every vowel. The name of the character Fiorello [*Il barbiere di Siviglia*] offers a simple example. Instead of singing Fiorello with a kind of American "*y*" as "*Fyore-lo*", you had to sing it as it looks, pronouncing the two first vowels distinctly, as "*Fiiiooorello*". Ubaldo's insistence on the importance of every vowel, consonant and syllable helped me to sing a smoother line. He would explain how attention to these tiny details would produce a more expressive and convincing performance. As a result, I've been told that I have a very communicative style when I sing Italian.

'During the rehearsal process Ubaldo often changed his mind, and, yes, it could be frustrating. But that became irrelevant. Maybe he saw something that we couldn't and decided it wasn't working. Sometimes he would just stop, and say, "Let's do it again", without explaining why. But Woody Allen, the movie director, is said to be exactly the same. If something's going wrong we've got to try it another way.

'Preparing an opera is a collaboration, it shouldn't be a dictatorship. For me the performance has to come from within, it has to be organic, otherwise it's not right and can feel mechanical. I think, too, in a sense, Ubaldo himself was performing, day in and day out. His changes of mind frequently produced new and better ways to get the production up another notch.

'Underpinning all the intensity of the work together was his belief in you. To draw out of you what he felt the phrase needed, he would sort of mime how to do it, breathing with you. If you are open to learning from him, it doesn't matter what he looks like, or how he grimaces.

'After Japan and my work with Ubaldo I went to study in Florence. His influence was such that even in ordinary, everyday communication I felt Italian. More recently I worked on another version of *Madama Butterfly* with a coach who told me that when I perform he can hear I'm not just singing notes, but that I have something concrete to express. That's the result of my induction into the correct way of singing in Italian and an apt tribute to Ubaldo's training.'

LILLIAN WATSON

SOPRANO

...as Ismène, *Mitridate, Re di Ponto* (Mozart), Royal Opera House Covent Garden

Lillian Watson is regarded as an exceptional coloratura soprano. Her astonishing vocal agility has led to worldwide concert and opera engagements, in repertoire ranging from Mozart to Strauss and Britten.

She is internationally known for her portrayal of Blonde (*Die Entführung aus dem Serail*) in acclaimed performances all under Sir Georg Solti, at Glyndebourne, the Royal Opera House Covent Garden and the Salzburg Festival. She has also recorded the role with Nikolaus Harnoncourt. Her other interpretations include the title role in Janácek's *The Cunning Little Vixen* (performed and recorded for EMI under Sir Simon Rattle); Titania in *A Midsummer Night's Dream* (Rome, Naples); *Capriccio* (Turin); Despina in *Così fan tutte* (Vienna, the Royal Opera House Covent Garden, Glyndebourne, Aix-en-Provence, Santa Fe and the Lincoln Center, New York); and both Ismène and Aspasia in *Mitridate, Re di Ponto* (Venice, Paris, London). A renowned interpreter of Richard Strauss's demanding soprano repertory, her successes have included Sophie in *Der Rosenkavalier* under Jeffrey Tate.

Recent operatic appearances include reprising the role of Despina (*Così fan tutte*) in new productions at English National Opera, Garsington Opera, the Lincoln Center and Santa Fe Opera.

Lillian Watson worked on the following roles with Ubaldo Gardini: Barbarina (Le Nozze di Figaro, *both for stage and recording), Despina* (Così fan tutte) *and Gianetta* (L'elisir d'amore), *all at the Royal Opera House Covent Garden. He also prepared her for recordings including Monteverdi Madrigals* (Leppard) *and* L'elisir d'amore (*Pritchard*).

'Coaches can have a huge effect on one's career. I feel I learned so much from Ubaldo. I first met him while I was still a student and working on Raymond Leppard's Monteverdi recordings. He was the language coach – the first I'd ever worked with – and it was partly thanks to him that I made my debut at Covent Garden and also began my recording work. Otherwise, it might have taken me longer to become established.

'While preparing Barbarina in *Le Nozze di Figaro*, which isn't a big part at all, I observed how Ubaldo dealt with the other singers, especially Susanna. When I went on to play that role myself, I realised how much I had learned simply by being around him.

'Ubaldo's love for and understanding of the human voice was obvious. He regarded each singer as an individual and made their distinctive qualities the basis of his work. You found what suited *your* voice and personality. You did it your way. He was very open, no question of him having one fixed idea and dictating "that's how it should be done".

'He also showed us that to build any role you must start with the text, be clear in what you're saying, why you're saying it, who you're saying it to. Only then can it be integrated with the music.

'I think one of the things that has actually held me in good stead, and that I teach rigidly now, is the Italianate way of singing – especially those wonderful, pure vowels. Many people sort of stop the voice to make the consonants. Ubaldo taught me that you can sing on the vowels, and that however many consonants there are in a phrase, you've got to get straight to the vowels and vocalise on them. You flick the consonants in very quickly (like pegging on a washing line), because only then can the voice really flow through, singing from vowel to vowel.

'Another aspect on which he was helpful was how to alter difficult vowel sounds on top notes to make them more singable. You can't sing "ih" high up, on, let's say, a top C. So you have to do what we call modifying the vowels – almost to "eh". Then the sound is deeper, not so horizontal, nor squeezed and doesn't sound shrill. For example, you might have to change the word "*mio*", to something like "*mey-o*". But a lot of language coaches expect you to sing "*mio*" up there, and for some voices this can result in an ugly sound.

'Ubaldo was always totally involved, [he was] not just the language coach sitting over in the corner, popping up every now and again to fix something linguistic. Of course, he understood that the director had the final say. But, through the language, by the time of the first major rehearsal he had planted so many seeds about the character that you went well equipped with lots of ideas to create your role.'

APPENDICES

Discography & Bibliography

DISCOGRAPHY

This list includes the principal recordings with which Ubaldo Gardini has been associated, either in his official capacity as Italian coach or for the preparation of individual artists. Many of the opera productions he coached were also filmed for television and video. He also featured in documentaries such as the BBC's *Call Me Flicka* and *Preparing an Opera*.

(Sources: Muze Classical Catalogue, (2007, unless otherwise stated), Gramophone Magazine, British Library Sound Archive (www.bl.uk/collections/sound-archive/cat.html))

Bellini	*Norma*	Caballé, Domingo, Cossotto, Raimondi, Collins, Bainbridge	Carlo Felice Cillario	Ambrosian Opera Chorus, London Philharmonic Orchestra	RCA	GD 86502
Bellini	*Norma*	Scotto, Troyanos, Murray, Crook, Giacomini, Plishka	James Levine	Ambrosian Opera Chorus, National Philharmonic Orchestra	SONY	SM2K 35902
Bellini	*I Puritani di Scozia*	Sutherland, Pavarotti, Cappuccilli, Ghiaurov, Caminada, Luccardi, Cazzaniga	Richard Bonynge	Royal Opera House Chorus, London Symphony Orchestra	DECCA	417 588-2DH3
Bellini	*La sonnambula*	Sutherland, Pavarotti, Ghiaurov, Jones, Buchanan, Tomlinson, de Palma	Richard Bonynge	London Opera Chorus, National Philharmonic Orchestra	DECCA	417 424-2DH2
Cilèa	*Adriana Lecouvreur*	Scotto, Domingo, Milnes, Obra't'sova, Luccardi, Andreolli, Hudson, Watson, Crook	James Levine	Philharmonia Orchestra, Ambrosian Opera Chorus,	CBS	CD 79310

Donizetti	*L'elisir d'amore*	Carteri, Alva, Panerai, Taddei, Vercelli	Tullio Serafin	La Scala Milan Chorus, La Scala Milan Orchestra	EMI	565658-2
Donizetti	*L'elisir d'amore*	Sutherland, Pavarotti, Cossa, Malas, Casula	Richard Bonynge	Ambrosian Singers, English Chamber Orchestra	DECCA	414 461-2DH2
Donizetti	*L'elisir d'amore*	Cotrubas, Domingo, Wixell, Evans, Watson	John Pritchard	Royal Opera House Covent Garden Chorus & Orchestra	SONY	M2K79210
Donizetti	*Lucia di Lammermoor*	Caballé, Carreras, Sardinero, Ramey, Murray, Ahnsjö, Bello	Jesús López-Cóbos	Ambrosian Opera Chorus, New Philharmonia Orchestra	Philips	426 563-2PM2 (2005 Catologue)
Donizetti	*Lucia di Lammermoor*	Sutherland, Pavarotti, Milnes, Ghiaurov, Touranjeau, Davies, Poli	Richard Bonynge	Royal Opera House Covent Garden Chorus & Orchestra	DECCA	410 193-2DH3
Donizetti	*Lucrezia Borgia*	Sutherland, Aragall, Wixell, Horne, Clark, de Palma, Visser, Bröcheler, Ewer, Van Allan, Zaccaria, Wilson-Johnson, Taylor	Richard Bonynge	National Philharmonic Orchestra, London Opera Chorus	DECCA	421 497-2DM2
Giordano	*Andrea Chénier*	Domingo, Scotto, Milnes, Sénéchal, Kraft, Ewing, Monk, Sharpe, Harling, Bushkin, King, de Palma, Beavan, Killebrew, Dara	James Levine	John Alldis Choir, National Philharmonic Orchestra	RCA	74321 39499-2

Handel	*Ariodante*	Baker, Mathis, Burrowes, Bowman, Rendall, Ramey, Oliver	Raymond Leppard	London Voices, English Chamber Orchestra	Philips	442 096-2PM2 (2005 Catalogue)
Mascagni	*Cavalleria rusticana*	Scotto, Domingo, Elvira, Kraft, Jones	James Levine	Ambrosian Opera Chorus, National Phil-harmonic Orchestra	RCA	74321 39500-2
Montemezzi	*L'amore dei tre re*	Moffo, Siepi, Domingo, Elvira, Davies, Tomkinson, Byers, MacGregor, Bainbridge, Sanderson	Nello Santi	Ambrosian Opera Chorus, London Symphony Orchestra	RCA	74321 50166-2
Monteverdi	*Il ritorno d'Ulisse in patria*	Von Stade, Condò, Stillwell, Cosotti, Parker, Murray, Lewis, Oliver, Power, Trama, Dickerson, Fryatt, Powell, Lewis, Bryson	Raymond Leppard	Glyndebourne Festi-val Opera Orchestra	CBS	79332 (Glyndebourne Recording, vinyl)
Monteverdi	The Book of Madrigals: III, IV, VII, VIII, IX	Luxon, Lloyd, Armstrong, Kern, Davies, Howells, Watson, Tear, Dean *et al.*	Raymond Leppard	English Chamber Orchestra	Philips	ASIN: B00000C2FB
Mozart	*La clemenza di Tito*	Baker, Popp, von Stade, Minton, Burrows, Lloyd	Colin Davis	Royal Opera House Covent Garden Chorus & Orchestra	Philips	422 544-2PME2 (2005 Catalogue)

Mozart	*Così fan tutte*	Caballé, Baker, Cotrubas, Gedda, Ganzarolli, Van Allan	Colin Davis	Royal Opera House Covent Garden Chorus & Orchestra	Philips	456 375-2PB8
Mozart	*Don Giovanni*	Wixell, Arroyo, Te Kanawa, Freni, Burrows, Ganzarolli, Van Allan, Roni	Colin Davis	Royal Opera House Covent Garden Chorus & Orchestra	Philips	456 375-2PB9
Mozart	*Don Giovanni*	Titus, Varady, Auger, Mathis, Moser, Panerai, Scholze, Rootering	Rafael Kubelík	Bavarian Radio Chorus and Symphony Orchestra	RCA	74321 25284-2
Mozart	*Don Giovanni*	Sramek, Weikl, Bacquier, Moll, Popp, Price, Burrows, Sass	Georg Solti	London Opera Chorus and Orchestra	Decca	ASIN: B00006469K
Mozart	*Don Giovanni*	Allen, Vaness, Ewing, Gale, Lewis, Van Allan, Rawnsley, Kavrakos	Bernard Haitink	Glyndebourne Festival Chorus, London Philharmonic Orchestra	EMI	747037-8 (2005 Catalogue)
Mozart	*Idomeneo*	Rinaldi, Shirley, Tear, Davies, Tinsley, Pilley, Dean	Colin Davis	BBC Symphony Chorus and Orchestra	Philips	420 130-2PH3
Mozart	*Idomeneo*	Von Stade, Behrens, Cotrubas, Pavarotti, Jenkins	James Levine	The Metropolitan Opera House New York Chorus & Orchestra	Deutsche Gramophon	073 4234GH2
Mozart	*Le Nozze di Figaro*	Titus, Donath, Furlanetto, Varady, Schmiege, Kallisch, Nimsgern	Colin Davis	Bavarian Radio Chorus and Symphony Orchestra	Philips	422 540-2PME3

Mozart	*Le Nozze di Figaro*	Van Dam, Popp, Hendricks, Raimondi, Baltsa, Palmer, Lloyd, Baldin, Jenkins, Maxwell, Pope	Neville Marriner	J. Constable, Ambrosian Opera Chorus, Academy of St. Martin-in-the-Fields	Philips	475 61118
Mozart	*Le Nozze di Figaro*	Ramey, Popp, Allen, Te Kanawa, Von Stade, Berbié, Moll, Tear, Langbridge, Tadeo, Kenny	Georg Solti	London Opera Chorus, London Philharmonic Orchestra	DECCA	410 150-2DH3
Mozart	*Le Nozze di Figaro*	Norman, Freni, Wixell, Minton, Ganzarolli, Tear, Casula, Grant, Lennox, Hudson, Watson	Colin Davis	BBC Symphony Chorus & Orchestra	Philips	456 375-2PB9
Puccini	*La Bohème*	Ricciarelli, Carreras, Putnam, Wixell, Hagegărd, Lloyd, de Angelis	Colin Davis	Royal Opera House Covent Garden Chorus & Orchestra	Philips	442 260-2PM2
Puccini	*La Bohème*	Caballé, Domingo, Blegen, Milnes, Sardinero, Raimondi, Mangin, Castel, Byers, Mason, Whiteley,	Georg Solti	Wandsworth School Boys' Choir, John Alldis Choir, London Philharmonic Orchestra	RCA	74321 39496-2
Puccini	*La Bohème*	Scotto, Kraus, Neblett, Milnes, Manuguerra, Plishka, Tajo, Capecchi, Crook, Lewis, Noble	James Levine	Trinity Boys Choir, Ambrosian Opera Chorus, National Philharmonic Orchestra	EMI	574985 2 (2005 catalogue)

Puccini	*La fanciulla del West*	Domingo, Milnes, Lloyd, Howell, Summers, Dobson, Crook, Leggate	Zubin Mehta	Royal Opera House Covent Garden Chorus & Orchestra	Deutsche Gramophon	419640 2GH2 (2005 catalogue)
Puccini	*Madama Butterfly*	Scotto, Domingo, Wixell, Knight, Andreolli, Summers, Muray, King, Keyte, Byers	Lorin Maazel	Ambrosian Opera Chorus, Philharmonia Orchestra	SONY	M2K35181
Puccini	*Suor Angelica*	Sutherland, Ludwig, Collins, Connell, Hartel, Buchanan, McLaughlin *et al.*	Richard Bonynge	Finchley Children's Music Group, The London Opera Chorus, National Philharmonic Orchestra	DECCA	458 218-2DM (2005 catalogue)
Puccini	*Tosca*	Caballé, Carreras, Wixell, Ramsey, de Palma, Trimarchi, Elvin, Muray	Colin Davis	Royal Opera House Covent Garden Chorus & Orchestra	Philips	464 729-2PM2
Puccini	*Le Villi*	Nucci, Scotto, Domingo, Gobbi	Lorin Maazel	Ambrosian Opera Chorus, National Philharmonic Orchestra	SONY	MK 76890 (2005 catalogue)
Rossini	*Il barbiere di Siviglia*	Sills, Milnes, Gedda, Capecchi Raimondi, Barbieri, Rippon, Galiano	James Levine	London Symphony Orchestra, John Alldis Choir	EMI	585523-2
Rossini	*Il barbiere di Siviglia*	Allen, Baltsa, Araiza, Trimarchi, Lloyd, Burgess, Best	Neville Marriner	Ambrosian Opera Chorus, Academy of St. Martin-in-the-Fields	Philips	446 448-2PH2 (2005 Catalogue)

Rossini	*Mosè in Egitto*	Raimondi, Anderson, Gal, Browne, Fisichella, Palacio, Lewis, Nimsgern	Claudio Scimone	Ambrosian Opera Chorus, Philharmonia Orchestra	Philips	420 109-2PM2 (2004 Catalogue)
Rossini	*Otello*	Carreras, Von Stade, Pastine, Fisichella, Condò, Ramey, Lewis, Leoz	Jesús López-Cóbos	Ambrosian Opera Chorus, Philharmonia Orchestra	Philips	475 448-2PM2
Verdi	*Attila*	Raimondi, Milnes, Cassinelli, Deutekom, Bastin, Bergonzi	Lamberto Gardelli	Royal Philharmonic Orchestra, Ambrosian Singers, Finchley Children's Music Group	DECCA	475 676-6PM2
Verdi	*Un ballo in maschera*	Caballé, Carreras, Wixell, Howell, Gharazian, Lloyd, Payne, Summers, Leggate, Elvin	Colin Davis	Royal Opera House Covent Garden Chorus & Orchestra	DECCA	470 586-2D0C2
Verdi	*Il corsaro*	Caballé, Carreras, Norman, Noble, Mastromei, Grant, Oliver	Lamberto Gardelli	Ambrosian Singers, New Philharmonia Orchestra	Philips	426 118-2PM2 (2005 Catalogue)
Verdi	*La forza del destino*	Price, Domingo, Milnes, Giacotti, Cossotto, Bacquier, Sénéchal, Moll	James Levine	John Alldis Choir, London Symphony Orchestra	RCA	74321 39502-2
Verdi	*Un giorno di regno*	Ganzarolli, Carreras, Cossotto, Wixell, Norman, Sardinero	Lamberto Gardelli	Ambrosian Singers, Royal Philharmonic Orchestra	Philips	492202

Verdi	*I Lombardi alla prima crociata*	Deutekom, Domingo, Raimondi, Lo Monaco, Dean, Grant, Aparici, Erwen, Malvisi	Lamberto Gardelli	Ambrosian Singers, Royal Philharmonic Orchestra	Philips	422 420-2PM2
Verdi	*Luisa Miller*	Ricciarelli, Domingo, Bruson, Howell, Ganzarolli, Obraztsova, Michael, de Corato	Lorin Maazel	Royal Opera House, Covent Garden, Chorus & Orchestra	Deutsche Gramophon	423 144-2GH2
Verdi	*I masnadieri*	Caballé, Bergonzi, Cappuccilli, Raimondi, Sandor, Mazzieri, Elvin	Lamberto Gardelli	Gardelli Ambrosian Singers, New Philharmonia Orchestra	Philips	475 8703
Verdi	*Otello*	Domingo, Scotto, Milnes, Little, Crook, Kraft, Plishka, King	James Levine	Ambrosian Opera Chorus, National Philharmonic Orchestra	RCA	74321 39501-2
Verdi	*Rigoletto*	Milnes, Sutherland, Pavarotti, Talvela, Tourangeau	Richard Bonynge	Ambrosian Opera Chorus, London Symphony Orchestra	DECCA	414 269-2DH2
Verdi	*La Traviata*	Cotrubas, Domingo, Milnes, Malagù, Jungwirth	Carlos Kleiber	Bavarian State Opera Chorus & Orchestra	Deutsche Gramophon	415 132-2GH2
Verdi	*La Traviata*	Sutherland, Pavarotti, Manuguerra, Gardini, Jones, Lambriks, Oliver, Tadeo, Summers, Elvin, Tomlinson, Wilson-Johnson	Richard Bonynge	London Opera Chorus, National Philharmonic Orchestra	DECCA	430 491-2DH2

Verdi	*Il Trovatore*	Ricciarelli, Carreras, Earle, Mazurok, Lloyd, Toczyska, Cannan, Treleaven	Colin Davis	Royal Opera House Covent Garden Chorus & Orchestra	Philips	446 151-2PM2 (2002 Catalogue)
Verdi	*Il Trovatore*	Pavarotti, Sutherland, Wixell, Horne, Ghiaurov, Burrowes	Richard Bonynge	London Opera Chorus, National Philharmonic Orchestra	DECCA	417 137-2DH2
Verdi	*I vespri Siciliani*	Arroyo, Sharpe, Domingo, Milnes, Ewing, Raimondi, Van Allan, Goeke, Collins, Morris, Byers	James Levine	John Alldis Choir, New Philharmonia Orchestra	RCA	09026 63492-2

BIBLIOGRAPHY

(published in London unless otherwise noted)

Adam, Nicky. *Who's Who in British Opera*: Scolar Press, 1993.

Alighieri, Dante. *The Divine Comedy*, translated by Allen Mandelbaum: Everyman Library, 1995.

Baker, Janet. *Full Circle (An Autobiographical Journey)*: Book Club Association, 1982.

Bret, David. *Maria Callas, The Tigress and the Lamb*: Robson Books, 1997.

Brooks, Thomas R. *The War North of Rome June 1944–May 1945*: Da Capo Press, 1996.

Castel, Nico. *Operatic Libretti Series*: Leyerle Publications, New York, 1990 ff.

Catford, J. C. *A Practical Introduction to Phonetics*: Oxford University Press, 1988, 1994, 2001.

Clivio, Gianrenzo. P. and Danesi, Marcel. *The Sounds, Forms, and Uses of Italian, an Introduction to Italian Linguistics*: University of Toronto Press, Canada, 2000.

Colorni, Evelina. *Singers' Italian: A Manual of Diction and Phonetics*: Wadsworth Publishing, 1970.

Cruttenden, Alan, ed. *Gimson's Pronunciation of English*: Hodder Arnold, 2001.

Fleming, Renée. *The Inner Voice: the making of a singer*: Penguin, 2004, 2005.

Gilbert, Susie and Shir, Jay. *A Tale of Four Houses*: HarperCollins Publishers, 2003.

Glendening, P. J. T. *Colloquial Handbooks: Italian*: Cassell, 1980.

Gobbi, Tito. *On His World of Italian Opera: Franklin* Watts, New York, 1984.

Harries, Meirion and Harries, Susie. *Opera Today*: Michael Joseph Ltd, 1986.

Hughes, Spike. *Glyndebourne: A History of the Festival Opera*: David & Charles, 1981.

Jones, Tobias. *The Dark Heart of Italy*: Faber & Faber, 2003.

Kimbell, David. *Italian Opera*: Cambridge University Press, 1991.

Lamb, Richard. *The War in Italy, 1943–1945: A Brutal Story*: John Murray, 1993.

Lenton, Sarah. *Backstage at the Opera*: Robson Books Ltd, 1998.

Lewis, Norman. *Naples,'44: A World War II Diary of Occupied Italy*: Carroll and Graf Publishers, New York, 1978 (published posthumously). (Also Collins, 1978 and Eland, 1983 and 2002).

Opera Guides [Various], *In association with English National Opera and The Royal Opera*: Calder Publications Ltd, 1980 ff (Series Editor: Nicholas John).

Osborne, Charles. *The Opera Lover's Companion*: Yale University Press, 2004.

Palmer, Andrew. *Divas In Their Own Words: Fifty Sopranos and Mezzo-Sopranos Talk About Their Voices and Careers*: The Vernon Press, Nottingham, 2000.

Pullum, Geoffrey K. and Ladusaw, William A. *Phonetic Symbol Guide*: The University of Chicago Press Ltd., 1996.

Robson, Mark. *Italy: Liberalism and Fascism* 1870–1945 (*Access to History*): Hodder Murray, 2000.

Sachs, Harvey. *Music in Fascist Italy*: Weidenfeld and Nicolson, 1987.

Snowman, Daniel. *The Hitler Emigrés: The Cultural Impact on Britain of Refugees from Nazism*: Pimlico, 2002.

Steane, J. B. *Singers of the Century* (3 vols): Duckworth & Co. Ltd., 2000.

Terkel, Studs. *And They All Sang*: Granta Books, 2006.

Thubron, Colin. *Royal Opera House in Covent Garden*: Hamish Hamilton, 1982.

Tooley, John. *In House: Covent Garden 50 years*: Faber & Faber, 1999.